PRAISE

Oh, to have had books like this when I was a teenager! What a wonderful, pure, heart-gripping, yet intriguingly adventurous journey. I relived my life all over again through thirteen-year-old Maggie, with her inquisitiveness, her seeing and wanting truth in all situations (unless she was at fault), spying on the weird neighbors next door and their even weirder fifteen-year-old son Ben, and possessing the typical teenage mouth that spouts off when she should be biting her tongue. Yet, our 1960's era heroine is ever respectful and considerate of her parents and has an uncompromising conviction of right and wrong. How privileged we are to be the speck on the wall inside Maggie's tree house and eavesdrop on someone so like ourselves.

J. Ledford Hamilton took us to a far more challenging place, though, than the innocent little tree house getaway and the juvenile spying. We were taken craftily and unsuspectingly into the dark side of prejudice and bigotry, where black is not black and white is not white, but, rather, where truth, justice and the American way are smeared with the grays of prejudicial graffiti. We find ourselves thrust into a world, which although few thankfully never enter, is nonetheless altogether real. It's a world where power and wealth and hatred for an entire people group boggles the mind of our innocent, trusting Maggie, who sees things quite clearly and somehow can't balance the operating dual standards which run dangerously contrary to her personal Christian beliefs.

L'Chaim ... To Life! is cleverly written, captivatingly compelling, and holds the reader from the opening page to story's end. It is a book you will not want to put down, but dreaded even more than reading interruptions is the inevitable end. The sequel cannot come soon enough!

—Diane A. McNeil, Author of
Ruth: 3,000 Years of Sleeping Prophecy Awakened

L'CHAIM

TO LIFE!

L'CHAIM

TO LIFE!

J. LEDFORD
HAMILTON

TATE PUBLISHING & Enterprises

Published by Tate Publishing & Enterprises, LLC
127 E. Trade Center Terrace | Mustang, Oklahoma 73064 USA
1.888.361.9473 | www.tatepublishing.com

Tate Publishing is committed to excellence in the publishing industry. The company reflects the philosophy established by the founders, based on Psalm 68:11,
"The Lord gave the word and great was the company of those who published it."

Book design copyright © 2011 by Tate Publishing, LLC. All rights reserved.
Cover design by Lauran Levy
Interior design by Chelsea Womble

Published in the United States of America

ISBN: 978-1-61777-207-8
1. Fiction, Coming of Age
2. Fiction, Cultural Heritage
11.03.18

This book is dedicated to the surviving children, grandchildren, nieces and nephews, brothers and sisters, aunts, uncles, and cousins of Holocaust victims, if there are any to be found. May we always remember (*zakar*, in Hebrew means "to make mention of") and never forget. And…

'YVAREKH'KHA ADONAI V'YISHMEREKHA.
(May the Lord bless you and keep you.)

YÄE R ADONAI PANAV ELEIKHA VICHUNEKKA.
(May the Lord make his face shine upon you
and show you his favor.)

YISSA ADONAI PANAV ELEIKHA V'YASEM I'KHA SHALOM.
(May the Lord lift up his face toward you and
give you peace.)

B'MIDBAR 6:24–26
(Numbers) 6:24–26

—*Complete Jewish Bible Translation*
(Old and New Testament) by David H. Stern

ACKNOWLEDGMENTS

I want to thank my heavenly Father who planted in my heart the love he has for his children Isra'el. Because he loves us so, he sent his only begotten son, Yeshua ha Mashiach, Jesus the Messiah, to bring us, his lost sheep, back into his fold.

To the staff at Tate Publishing. You are the epitome of dream catchers. It's as if you caught in midair the dream I'd had of someday becoming a writer, breathed life into it, and made it so. But how you take my rambling thoughts and turn them into a readable book is beyond me. You have set my feet on the path that my Lord had already designed just for me, and I thank you.

I want to thank my parents, William P. and Dorothy Ledford, for taking such good care of me from the time I came to live with them in 1956 after my birth parents passed away. I was seven years old. It has been my goal to pass on to my children and grandchildren the values and life lessons instilled in me by these two selfless people.

I want to thank my wonderful and generous husband and best friend, Jerry Hamilton, who has never told me no. Never, not once! You look at me through rose-colored glasses, and I hope for my sake you never take them off!

To my sons, Jim, Kevin, Darin, Robbie, and Ryan. You have always made me proud to be your mom; and to those of you who have served our country in the navy, air force, and army, your faithfulness to go when called has lifted our little family band to a higher standard to which I am honored to be a part. To my sons-in-law, Steven and Jeff, thank you for taking good care of my girls.

To my daughters, Lisa and Jerri Dell, and daughters-in-law Saundra, Kristy, Heather 1 and Heather 2, you are exactly what I always wished I could be—extraordinary!

To my nineteen beautiful grandchildren, Emberly, Mikayla, Stephenie, Jared, Kaitlin, Zack, Brandon, Charity, Blake, Maddie Grace, Ethan, Kayla, Trey, Jill,

Jacob, Logan, Kira, Kameryn, and Kylie. It's funny how we always thought our kids were the cutest kids on earth until they grew up and had kids! There's no comparison! (Sorry, guys, but it's true.)

To the precious new addition to our family, our first great-grandchild, Hadlee Marie. You must feel like the little red caboose!

To my sister Linda Ledford, who has always encouraged me to keep the faith. Life hasn't always been so easy for us and sometimes not even so good, but we have always been there for each other. That's what sisters do.

To my alumni friends and classmates from SDHS, Homestead, Florida. Go Rebs!

A special thanks to my long lost friends Linda and Greg Lilge, just because you said I could do this!

A special thanks to Kaitlin Mardis, Ken Roberts, Glenna Jackson, and Lynn Shelton for their expertise in proofreading and their patience with a very excited babbling idiot of a first-time writer.

And last but not least, to my brother, Gary Ledford. Your love for the Father and the Hebrew language has been such a blessing to me as well as a tremendous help. All of your study and research has finally paid off, and all I ever had to do was pour you a cup of coffee and sit down and listen. You're amazing.

These people have all contributed in one way or another in making this book into the story that it was meant to be.

In collecting materials needed to make this story a fiction based on fact kind of story, I want to acknowledge the many helps that came my way. The first and most valuable source of truth is of course the Bible, and although from my youth the King James Version was the most readily available, I became aware of other translations later on that were equally helpful in increasing my understanding of scripture. One of these is *The Complete Jewish Bible* by David H. Stern. It is with this version that I discovered the invaluable method of reading scriptures used by many of the Jewish people.

Brad Scott from Wildbranch Ministries is a truly gifted teacher of the Hebrew language and a dear friend. His unique style and method of teaching opened my mind to hidden truths, warmed my heart to the love of the Father, taught me about the symbols of our faith, and made me laugh.

Chapter One

It didn't seem like anything at first, just a soft glow of light coming through the outstretched branches of the old oak tree beside our house. I stared hard into the darkness trying to make out details. *Was it six little individual lights?* I brushed my bangs back out of my eyes and stared again. *No, it's seven, I think. Yeah, seven.* A mosquito lit on the bony part of my elbow. *I could slap it off, ending its life for good, or sit here on the ledge and watch what happens.* I slapped it hard, blood splattering on the inside of my palm. Wiping my hand across my tee shirt before grabbing a handful of bangs again, I slumped forward to get a better look.

There were people walking around in the room casting shadows here and there on the walls and ceiling. Amused at the ability to entertain myself from my ring-side seat, I shifted slightly to the right, pulling my knees in closer to my chest and resting my chin on the ragged Band-Aid that covered a week-old skinned knee. A breeze blew across the front lawn, rustling the tall weeds next to the wooden fence that separated me from the strange light. I shivered. *Fall is coming. A chilling mystery full of suspense and mayhem is always better in the fall.* This was the third Friday night in a row that I had sat out here on the ledge of the porch roof secretly spying on my new neighbors. And every Friday night at about this time, the little room in the house on the other side of the wooden fence is all aglow with light and people. *Could be someone's birthday, but three in a row?* I glanced over my shoulder to check my own bedroom window, the one I had crawled through to get to my post on the roof. My little sister was sound asleep, and I was sure my parents would still be glued to the evening news on the radio. I turned my attention back to the light. It looked bigger now, almost as if it had suddenly become one, an all consuming fire instead of just a group of small separate ones.

I yawned, blinking my watery eyes. Staring was hard on my tired eyes, of course, and straining to see through the shadowy darkness to spy on my neighbors didn't help. I scanned the horizon, resting my weary eyes for a few minutes. *It's so peaceful up here, away from everyone and everything.* I contemplated crawling back inside to get a pillow and blanket and make this roof ledge my bed for the night.

Peeking over the edge to the sidewalk below, I spotted my old rusty red bicycle carelessly tossed aside in the grass ten feet beneath my perch. *Wonder how long that's been lying there? Judging from the height of the grass, I'd say at least three weeks. That's right, three weeks ago, the day the new neighbors arrived with their big U-Haul truck and a loaded-down dusty grey sedan.* I had jumped off my bike just in time to hide myself in the elderberry bush next to the porch. I wasn't too keen on meeting new people, at least not until I'd had time to check them out first. I had decided I would climb out onto the roof after supper and spy them out, which is how it happened that I saw the lights for the first time. Thinking about that now made it seem as if it were months ago.

I had heard my dad say the new tenant's name was Joe Davis and he had moved here from South Miami with his wife, Ruby, and their only son, Ben. Sounded normal enough to Dad, but then he didn't know about

15

these strange Friday night occurrences like I did. He was always pretty careful about who he rented the little white house to, especially since last year when that guy up and moved out in the middle of the night, with no word as to where Dad could meet him to collect the month's rent. My father was pretty sore about it and swore he'd be a lot more careful from then on. So I guessed he must have checked these people out pretty thoroughly before handing over the keys to the house. Being a landlord was a new thing for my father.

We had lived in this same neighborhood for as long as I could remember, although my mom says we first lived in an apartment in the city when I was born in 1949. They had bought the little house that we now rent out in 1952, which was perfect for the three of us, but it only had two bedrooms, which were quite small for our soon-to-be-growing family, so by 1955 they were looking for something bigger. It at least had to have a separate dining room, my mom had said. When our present house went up for sale in 1956, the same year my sister Elizabeth (Betsy for short) was born, we walked next door to take a look at it. Mom went crazy over the big, roomy kitchen and formal dining area, and Dad liked the fact that there was a garage, but what sold me on it was the big oak tree—huge and powerful, with limbs stretching all the way across the wooden fence into my own little backyard. Being forced to admire it from a distance, I knew that I would never get the chance to climb it because the whole trunk of the tree was in the wrong yard. The price must have been right because we didn't have to sell our little house to buy this one, and within just a few weeks we moved in. For the past six years we have lived on the trunk side of the fence, rendering the big tree all mine and making my dad a landlord.

Someone was standing on the front porch looking toward my house. I ducked down the best I could. *Did he see me?* I raised my head just enough to check out the stranger. He was now turned to the side, and I could see that he was wearing a cap of some kind, small, and barely covering the top of his head. Tracing the path of the direction he was now looking, my gaze fell upon the light inside the house, but now what I saw was one taller light in the center of what appeared to be three smaller lights on either side. I was mesmerized as I stared at the lights, no longer concerned with the stranger standing on the porch. I didn't care if he saw me or not; I only knew I couldn't take my eyes off those lights. Then suddenly a shadow appeared, and the lights were gone. It was over. I sat dumbfounded on my ledge, wondering what it all meant.

Slowly I crept back through the little clerestory window, climbing over the blanket chest that sat on the floor beneath the window sill. Filled with wonder and awe of what I had seen, I reached for my pajamas from under my pillow and headed down the hall to the bathroom.

CHAPTER TWO

It's hard to find time to be alone in a house full of stuff that always needs to be done. My mom was number one at finding things for me to do on a Saturday so she and my father could go into the city to shop. What I really wanted to do was get off by myself and think. At thirteen, I had a lot on my mind. Eighth grade was a pretty big deal in junior high; there were new kids to meet, of course, and there were boys, something I was uneasy about. Not that I thought I would have a problem with boys, or boyfriends, for that matter, but I knew they liked it when the girls were weak and help-less, two things that I was determined never to be. I glanced into the mirror over my parents' dresser at my own reflection: *not bad looking or homely exactly, but kind of plain. I could try wearing my hair in a more fashionable style instead of this ponytail and bangs,* I thought. *Maybe I should get it cut in the new pageboy style I had seen in Mom's latest fashion magazine.* I walked over closer to the mirror, taking in my full face and figure. *With my hair pulled back like this, I barely even look like a girl,* I thought, as my eyes traveled down to my chest. *Besides, if I don't start growing some girlie parts, there's no sense in wasting money on a fancy haircut!* I finished dusting the armoire and moved on to the dining room.

Why do people think they've got to have so much furniture? Eight chairs. *There's only four of us.* Three leaves in a table that stretched from one end of the room to the other, a china cabinet, a fancy serving cart, and that other thing with a bunch of lace tablecloths and napkin rings in it. *We never use any of this stuff,* I grumbled as I hastily wiped the cabinet down with furniture polish. We hardly ever sat at the table to eat but rather used the smaller red Formica dinette set in the kitchen that seated the four of us comfortably and never needed dusting. Rubbing the sweet lemon oil into the dark wood reminded me of my mother and made me smile in spite of myself. She was a very talented lady when it comes to furniture. She shopped thrift stores and rummage sales and came home with some of the ugliest-looking junk I've ever seen, only to refinish it herself, turning it into a superb piece of furniture—for me to keep dusted, of course.

I had taken over the chore of dusting our furniture at the age of five, and at thirteen I'm still at it. Betsy, on the other hand, came into this world doing absolutely nothing and has developed it into a fine art. Even at six years old you'd think there was something she could do to be helpful. But to my parents, Betsy was still the baby, and therefore little if anything was ever expected of her. So while I finished up the dusting and moved on to folding laundry, my sister sat on her bed upstairs combing her precious doll's hair, or playing with her new Fashion Queen Barbie, or rearranging her many, many dolls on the shelves above her headboard.

I was never one to actually play with dolls. I just couldn't see the point; it was like practicing for something that wasn't going to happen for a long, long time. However, I did at one time own an impressive collection of paper dolls—all famous movie stars and popular entertainers of the mid to late fifties. There were Pat Boone, Loretta Young, Gale Storm, The Lennon Sisters, Elvis, and my all-time favorites, Annette and the Mouseketeers. Naturally once I had outgrown these playthings, I graciously passed them on to Betsy, but dolls made of paper didn't interest her, so eventually they all went into the Salvation Army box that Mom carried to the drop-off center next to the Winn Dixie in town.

With all my self-righteous grumbling I had lost track of time, and before I knew it my chores were finished. Tossing the laundry basket into the bottom of the closet, I took off out the back door.

My best daytime post for spying on the neighbors was in the tree house. My dad had managed to come up with enough scrap lumber from around the neighborhood to build me a much-longed-for tree house in the limbs of the magnificent old oak. Covered with a thick canopy of low-hanging branches of pale green leaves, I felt fairly confident that I could go undetected for the remainder of the late summer afternoon. Seated on the old ragged boat cushion I had found in the garage right after we moved in, I rested my elbows carefully on the roughly cut lumber that framed out the little window facing the house of the weird ones, as I had decided to call them. No movement, I noticed, either inside or out. Nothing seems to be going on at all. It didn't take long for boredom to creep into my mind. *Good grief, what do these people do all day?* The car was in the drive-way, the kid's bike was leaning up against the house, and there were no lights on inside. Even their dog seemed disinterested in the fact that it was a bright, sunshiny Saturday afternoon. He was sleeping peace-fully, half in and half out of his dog house, the name Sparky painted over the entrance in big black letters. I gave a long, low whistle in the direction of the dog. His ears perked slightly and then drooped. *Dumb dog. If I had a dog, he'd be nothing like that. He would be smart and keen in sight and hearing, not lazy and good for nothing like that mutt.*

I was starting to get a little sleepy myself as a soft, warm breeze swirled around the old tree causing the leaves to rustle, sending little sparkles of filtered sun-light dancing on the walls of the tree house. I reached for my rolled-up sleeping bag that was stashed in the corner. *I'll rest for a minute or two and then check on the weird ones again.* As I unrolled the bag, the aroma of hickory smoke and pine from our last campout on the river filled the tiny room of the tree house, stirring memories of campfires and roasted marshmallows. *I wonder if weird boy next door ever goes camping,* I thought as I snuggled down into the warm bag. *Nah, I doubt he's the type,* I decided, as I drifted off.

"Maggie, I'm hungry, and Mommy's not home yet." I jumped at the sound of Betsy's voice. She was standing on the ladder looking into the tree house at me; she knew better than to enter uninvited—house rules.

I sat up and rubbed my eyes. My hair was matted and stuck to the side of my face; something white and gummy was protruding from the edge of my bangs. *Marshmallow!* I pulled at it with my fingernails, scraping it loose from my hair. "Here, eat this," I said dully, shoving my sticky fingers in her direction.

"Yucky! I don't want that! You're being mean, and I'm telling Mommy."

"I'm just messing with you, Betsy. Geez Louise, can't you take a joke?" I knew I'd be in big trouble if Mom found out I was sleeping in the tree house instead of keeping an eye on the kid as I was told to do before she and Dad left to get groceries. I was having a hard enough time convincing them that I was old enough to stay home alone; it wouldn't do for Betsy to tattle-tale on me. I started down the ladder after my little sister when I heard an unfamiliar voice coming from the other side of the fence.

"Hey," was all he said. Cautiously I peered around the massive tree trunk, my heart in my throat. I wasn't ready for a face-to-face encounter with one of the weird ones. I liked it better when I was the only one doing the looking.

"Hey, yourself," I mumbled awkwardly, swallowing hard to wash the creak from my voice. I felt that all too familiar heat rising in my cheeks. *Lord, please don't let me say anything stupid*, I begged. The boy wasn't fazed by my shyness. He smiled and then stuck his arm over the fence, extending his hand in a friendly manner. "Name's Ben. What's yours?" I didn't move. He continued to smile, a little less broad perhaps but still hopeful. A shadow caught the corner of my eye as Betsy approached the fence. She reached up for the stranger's hand.

"I'm Betsy, and she's Maggie," she said, nodding in my direction. "Nice to meet you, Ben."

I let go of the ladder and moved closer to the fence. I couldn't take my eyes off the boy's face. I had never seen anyone who looked like him. He was tall and slim, almost skinny, and dark headed. But it was his skin color that intrigued me, not tanned exactly, more like heavily creamed coffee, the way my daddy drank it; and he was still smiling. I moved a little closer, extending a guarded hand toward his.

"Nice to meet you, Maggie." His hands were smooth and refined; even his fingernails were immaculate, not rough and dirty like mine. I quickly pulled away, stuffing my hand into the back pocket of my blue jeans. His deeply haunting eyes met my stare with gentle persuasion. Nervously I looked at the ground, breaking the perpetual stare.

I knew better than to let my motor-mouth little sister start talking, so with every ounce of courage I could muster, I managed to open my mouth. "Yeah, you too." There it was—that uncomfortable, intimidating silence, adding to my already lack of social confidence.

"Come on, Betsy," I whispered, giving my sister a little push. "We gotta get inside."

"I'll see you later then," Ben called out cheerfully. I took Betsy by the arm and headed for the back door. I knew he was still standing by the fence watching us as we went inside the house. *Some spy you turned out to be*, I chided myself as I closed the screen door safely behind me. I hurried over to look out the kitchen window in the direction of the tree house, but Ben was nowhere in sight.

CHAPTER THREE

Mom and Dad came through the front door just as I was trimming the crust off Betsy's peanut butter and jelly sandwich. *Maybe if she's eating she won't run her mouth about Ben.* I poured her a glass of milk and went to help Mom put away the groceries. She was quiet, almost stifled it seemed, but I decided not to question her. *Maybe she and Dad had an argument or something. Well, whatever it is, it will pass.* My mother was not one to dwell on problems or hold a grudge. She always said life was too short to spend time being angry. It seemed to me that she lost a lot of arguments that way.

Daddy followed my mom through the dining room into the kitchen carrying the last of the grocery bags. Without a word, he sat the bags onto the counter and walked out to the back porch. Picking up a box of oatmeal, I turned toward the screen door just in time to see a silver thread of smoke curling around my father's head and disappearing into thin air. *He's smoking again, which he hasn't done for three years. This can't be good.*

"Mom—," I started, but she cut me off with a look that I had learned early on not to cross. I finished putting away the groceries for her as she stepped out onto the porch, putting her arm around my father.

"Ted, why does this have to be a problem?" she pleaded with him. "Can't we just let it go? There's nothing we can do about it now, so why not just leave them alone?" He didn't move. His chin was locked as he sucked hard on his cigarette. He was staring across the yard at the house next door. "Honey, what harm is there in letting them stay? After all, this is 1962; things are different now."

What did she mean, different? I moved closer to the back door, careful to stay out of sight. He didn't answer her; he just flicked his cigarette out into the grass and turned to come back into the house. I grabbed Betsy's empty glass and hurried to the sink, pretending to be busy cleaning up after her. Dad rushed past me and went into their bedroom, my mother right on his heels.

"You girls go in and turn the television on for a while, Maggie," Mom said, touching my shoulder gently as she followed Daddy into their room, closing the door behind her.

Betsy jumped up from the table, bread crumbs falling to the floor as she skipped down the hall to the living room. "Mickey Mouse Club is coming on, Maggie! Hurry up and fix the rabbit ears for me," she demanded. I obeyed the little troll only because I was anxious to hear more about "the problem." Getting Betsy settled in front of the TV only took a minute or two, and as soon as the program started, she was content. I slipped past the sofa where she sat and tiptoed to my parents' bedroom door.

"I can't do this, Marge; you know that!" He sounded furious. "If they had been up front about it to begin with, I would have never rented to them!" So this was about the weird ones! I knew it! I leaned closer. He was pacing around, stopping every now and then to pound his fist on the dresser. "How did this get past me? I'm smarter than that, Margie. Don't you think so? I mean, shouldn't I have picked up on something? Seen something strange? I thought those people dressed funny and carried around little scrolls or something. How was I to know?" Mom wasn't talking, at least not loud enough for me to hear.

It got quiet for a minute, and then I heard something like a sniffle coming from the other side of the door. *Mom must be crying,* I thought. *Man, I hate that!* "Marge, they're Jews," he yelled. "Jews! What am I going to do? You know if Charlie down at the plant finds out, it will get all over town! We'll be black-listed from now on!" More pacing and fist pounding. "Crap! I guess if the cashier at Winn Dixie knows, it's already all over town!" he shouted. "Why did this have to happen to us? Why?"

"Nothing has happened yet, Ted," my mother's tearful voice came soft and entreating. "They seem to be nice people, and besides, maybe they won't stay long, and this will all just blow over." That's my mom; optimistically blind-sided. *But why was Dad so upset that the weird ones were Jews? Big deal! The O'Malleys down the street were Irish, and that didn't seem to bother anyone. And what about the Perrys from up north somewhere? I think they are French or Swedish or something.*

"It has nothing to do with being nice," my dad said, a hint of genuine sadness in his voice, "They have to get out, regardless."

It was getting too still on the other side of the door, so I decided to back away quietly and retreat to the living room. Betsy was still glued to the television and didn't seem to notice that I was just now joining in. After a few minutes Mom and Dad came into the room and sat down.

Betsy jumped up and ran to Dad climbing into his lap. "We made a new friend today, Daddy; his name is Ben," she reported gleefully. "He lives right next door, and he's really nice; he even spoke first and shook hands and everything!" *I guess the weird one managed to make a good impression on somebody after all,* I mused.

Dad sat Betsy down roughly on the floor and then stood to his feet. "I don't want either of you girls to have any more to do with those people, you hear me?" *Because they're Jewish?* I wondered.

"But Daddy—," Betsy started to protest.

"No!" he shouted. That was it. He would not hear of it again. Mom sat staring down at her hands as Betsy began whimpering.

"It's okay, baby," Mom said. "Your daddy's just a little upset, that's all. It will be all right." She pulled Betsy into her lap, smoothing her hair and speaking softly. "Daddy is afraid that the new neighbors might be a bad influence on you girls, and he doesn't want that; so be good girls and do as he says, okay?"

"I don't know what the big deal is anyway," I remarked. "It's not as if we invited them over for dinner or anything. Good grief, Betsy, we just met him today, and personally I think he's weird and ugly, and I don't even want him for a friend." I knew I had lied, but it was the only thing I could think of to get Betsy to shut up about it and to reassure my mother that I wasn't planning on getting to know these new people. But deep down inside, I believed that there was something mysteriously intriguing about them, and the fact that my dad seemed bent on removing these people from the neighborhood made the idea of learning more about them all the more captivating.

Later that night as I sat out on the roof looking over at the little white house next door, I pondered the events of the evening. I had never met a Jew. To my knowledge I hadn't actually ever even seen a Jew.

I didn't know anything about Jews, and I couldn't say that I was especially interested in Jews, but my father's anger that they had tricked him into letting them move into our house caused an insatiable amount of curiosity in my mind. I determined right then and there that I would find a way to learn more about them without my parents getting suspicious and without getting myself into any unnecessary trouble. And, if they had tricked my father, why did they feel that it was necessary? Was there something about my own dad that I didn't know? Or, could it be that my dad actually has reasons for not trusting Jews? I had to learn the truth.

As I rose up onto my knees preparing to crawl back inside, I noticed a sliver of light coming from the direction of the tree house. *Who on earth would be snooping around my tree house at this hour?* I crouched forward to get a better look, but the big tree sat too far back in the yard and the corner of the house blocked my view. Quickly I scampered back into my room, peeked in on Betsy who was sleeping soundly, grabbed my bathrobe and hurried downstairs to the back door.

The beam of light was now moving across the neighbors' backyard. I was too late to catch my intruder.

As the light disappeared into the house, I quietly slipped out the back door and ran across the lawn to the tree house. Climbing the ladder, I suddenly realized how dark it was and that I didn't have a flashlight. Scrambling back down the ladder, I ran to the house to retrieve the flashlight my mother kept on a shelf over the washer on the back porch. After checking the batteries, I took off back across the yard to the tree house and climbed the ladder. Whoever had been out here earlier wasn't here now, so I knew I had nothing to be afraid of. Still, I had the uneasy feeling that I was being watched. *It's just my guilty conscience*, I determined, based on my own current devious activities.

Using the flashlight, I scanned the floor of the tree house without climbing any further. There was something over in the far corner that I knew didn't belong to me, nor did it belong in my tree house. I crawled across the floor to the corner and retrieved the strange object. I had never seen anything like it in my life, yet it was oddly familiar. Tucking the mysterious object into my bathrobe, I climbed down the ladder and walked back to the house, seeing from the corner of my eye the shadow of a teenage boy sitting on the steps of the back porch next door.

CHAPTER FOUR

Every now and then after church on Sunday, my family would have dinner with Mr. and Mrs. Catelli and their two children, twelve-year-old Maria and her five-year-old brother, William. I wasn't particularly fond of these kids, I think because they were so spoiled. They were rich by our standards and went to private school, but that wasn't really the problem. It was more about how they acted around other people that irked me; like they thought they were so much better than everyone else. But it was important to my father that we went and that we behaved ourselves properly.

Mr. Catelli was the owner of the fabrications plant where my father worked, and for some reason he had taken a special interest in my dad and started inviting us to their mansion high up on a hilltop, overlooking the Tennessee River. Mom was appreciative and gracious as always but seemed like a fish out of water to me. Still, she never complained; it wasn't her nature. She did, however, have a certain way of sticking up for her kids.

The first time we went wasn't so bad, except that when Mrs. Catelli told Maria to take me and Betsy out back to see the two-story playhouse, she refused, stomping her foot and declaring that she didn't allow outsiders in her playhouse. I thought that was pretty gutsy of her, although my mother said later that it was inexcusably rude and she was thankful that her own two girls would never treat a guest so outrageously.

The next visit to the Catelli home had the potential for disaster as well, primarily because my mother had informed my father that if there was a repeat of the unacceptable behavior and attitude displayed by that little miss fancy pants Maria (Mom's words exactly) toward her daughters, she and the girls would not be returning—ever. Lucky for Dad the Catelli children were away visiting cousins in Atlanta and would not be joining us for dinner. As it turned out, Betsy and I spent the better half of the afternoon in the extravagant two-room playhouse complete with child-sized furniture and a working electric fireplace, pretty fabulous even in my book. But the highlight of the entire day was watching Betsy strip, re-dress, and then rearrange all of Maria Catelli's dolls and stuffed animals to her liking. What a mess! It was great. I thought for sure we would never be invited back, but I was wrong.

I had tried to beg off from going to church, faking a headache, but to no avail. I wanted to do some investigating on my newly acquired treasure discovered in my tree house the night before. It was heavy for its size of only seven or eight inches high and had an unusual shape, like a tree maybe, except it was flatter and had odd markings on it. I still didn't know what it was, but with a little research using my World Book Encyclopedias, I was pretty sure I could find out. But it would have to wait hidden away safely in the back of my sock drawer. I thought about it all the way to church.

In my Sunday school class, some of the kids wanted to talk about the upcoming Pastor Appreciation Day picnic of which I was on the activities planning committee for the youth department. At this point, I was pretty sure I really did have a headache. I couldn't keep my mind on the discussion in the class, and on top of that, with the exception of the good food, I wasn't looking forward to dinner at the Catellis.' *Why couldn't they just let me stay home for once? It's not like I was denying the faith or becoming a heretic.* It was clear to me that my needs were not their top priority. I needed a break, and I would have to figure out how I was going to get one. In the meantime, food would meet an immediate need, and the Catellis had a good cook.

We arrived for dinner shortly before two o'clock, Mom and Dad being unusually quiet, Betsy chattering away about some Barbie doll nonsense, and me with a full-blown headache. We followed Mrs. Catelli into the massive, formal dining room and took our places at the table. Mr. Catelli looked troubled, his brow deeply furrowed. *Maybe something has given him a headache, too,* I thought. The pot roast smelled delicious, and as soon as William pronounced "amen" after his blessing, bowls and platters began revolving around the table. The cook retreated to the kitchen only to return moments later with a basket filled with piping hot yeast rolls and warm honey. I ate until I hurt and then ate some more. Still, Mr. Catelli had very little to say. My father seemed not to notice.

Later that afternoon while trying to find the bathroom, I stumbled into a very heated conversation between my father and Mr. Catelli. Neither of them saw me, so I quickly backed up three steps and hid myself behind the doorway of the study. Mr. Catelli was pacing back and forth in front of a big stained glass window, puffing hard on a cigar while my dad sat on the edge of the white brocade sofa, his head down and his fingers crisscrossed on the back of his neck. I remembered seeing him like that once before when my mother came home from a doctor's visit and announced that she had cancer. It turned out to be a false alarm, but my dad never got over it. It liked to have scared him to death. The pale tint in his skin and the tightness in his fingers told me that this might be equally as serious.

"Ted, you have got to put an end to this," Mr. Catelli was saying. "I can't have my employees thinking that my number one plant foreman rents his house to a stinking Jew. You are going to have to fix this, or else."

"I'm not the number one foreman, Mr. Catelli. Charlie Ross is. I'm just a line supervisor." He barely looked up when he said it.

"Maybe not, Ted, but if you handle this unfortunate situation correctly, a promotion could most likely be in the works." He continued pacing, blowing his smelly cigar smoke all over the room. "We have struggled long and hard to get this plant up and running since the end of the war, and I don't intend to let some little insignificant Jew interfere with our success." Mr. Catelli's choice of words he used to describe my next-door neighbors landed like a brick in the pit of my stomach. He walked over to my father and placed his hand on my dad's shoulder. "Ted, I have total confidence in you, and if it's the money that the old Jew pays to rent your house, I'll see to it that you are compensated for the full amount until you can find a more suitable tenant. You understand?"

My father rose slowly to his feet. "I'll take care of it, Mr. Catelli. You got my word on it." The sadness in his voice was heartbreaking. I wanted so badly to help him, but I was just a kid, and this problem seemed to be growing bigger and uglier than I could have imagined.

"That's the spirit, Teddy, my boy!" Mr. Catelli slapped him hard on the back. *Dad hates it when people call him that*, I thought. *It's so condescending.* He reached for my father's hand, giving it a firm shake. "It's settled then. Now, how about some of Mrs. Jacobsen's apple pie? You know, Ted, I had to pay a pretty penny to get her to stay on here as cook and housekeeper. Yes sir, when the misses and I foreclosed on this place back in 1954 from old man Jacobsen, his wife came to me begging for a job. What could I do? I knew they had fallen on hard times, but business is business, don't you agree?" He looked at my dad's face for confirmation but got nothing. "Well, anyway, I decided to give her a position as maid and housekeeper for my wife, and it wasn't too long before we discovered that she could cook. That's when her fee went up, but it was worth it. She's the best dad-burn cook in the South, I can tell you that. So how about some of that pie?" I quickly slipped out the side door to the patio where Betsy was playing in the garden with William. (She had been banned from the playhouse.)

We didn't get any pie. Dad was so distraught that he made up some excuse saying we had to leave right away. Mom stood talking quietly with Mrs. Catelli on the front lawn for a few minutes while we waited in the car. Dad was obviously in such a hurry to leave that he did something totally inexcusable in my mother's eyes—he blew the horn. Mom turned abruptly and walked quickly toward the car, a look of shock and disapproval on her face.

No one spoke for a good ten minutes. Betsy had drifted off to sleep and was taking up most of the back seat, but I didn't want to make a fuss, thinking this whole thing could turn ugly at the least little thing, so I crunched up against the door and turned to look out the side window. I would wait for one of them to break the silence. My dad went first.

"He says I gotta get rid of the Jews, Marge. I'm afraid if I don't do something quick I could lose my job over this. It's serious, Margie, real serious." Suddenly he slammed his palms against the steering wheel in protest. "God, why did this have to happen! All that praying we do, and look where it gets us! Geez!"

Mom glanced over her seat at her sleeping child, and then gently touched my father's shoulder. "Ted, try to stay calm, honey, so we don't upset the children." She looked back at me and smiled. "Didn't you have a nice time today, Maggie, dear? I thought you kids got along much better, and that William is just the sweetest little thing."

"Mom, I'm not a baby; I know what's going on. I heard Mr. Catelli talking to Dad about the Jews." My mother turned pale with shock as she slowly looked back at my father. "I just don't see why it's anybody's business who we rent our house to. Does Mr. Catelli even know these people? I mean, come on, Mom, you can see that the Catellis are snobs and their kids are brats. Why does it matter what they think about us or our neighbors?"

"What matters, young lady, is that Mr. Catelli is my boss, and if he says that someone has to go, then they have to go! It's that simple!" Dad was furious, and I was fixing to catch the raw end of the stick. "You don't know about Jews, how they are. They cheat people, they steal, lie; you name it! We can't have that kind of trash in our neighborhood around our kids!" He had a white-knuckled death grip on the steering wheel. "By God, I'll burn that house to the ground before I let some Jew ruin the neighborhood!" he shouted. *Were these vile and repulsive words those of my father's or the words of Mr. Catelli? It didn't sound like my father.* Betsy sat up, looking as if she had just had a bad dream. Mom turned to look out the window, chewing nervously on her fingernails.

"Okay, Dad, I get it!" I shouted back at him. "No Jews allowed!" I didn't even know why I was defending them. I was surprised to realize that it even mattered to me at all. I just didn't like other people telling my folks what they could and couldn't do. After all, this was America—land of the free, home of the brave! *But don't Jewish people have just as much right to be free in America?*

My father lowered his voice as he began talking to Mom. I had to lean up in my seat to hear what he was saying. It seemed that in a little over three weeks, word had gotten out about the Jews living in our rental house. Suddenly we were important in the neighborhood. That thought humored me. *If the cashier at Winn Dixie knew we had Jews living right next door, what next? The barber? The PTA? The guy who pumps our gas?* I chuckled softly to myself as I pictured my proud parents standing in line at the grocery store while some little miss nosey told them what she knew. *Boy, I bet that ticked him off! Any time a cashier knows your business before you do, it can't be good.* We pulled into the driveway, no one daring to look in the direction of the little white house.

CHAPTER FIVE

All evening I kept having one reoccurring thought: *Somebody should warn the Jews. It's not right that they don't know what people are saying about them. Maybe they would want to fight back, defend themselves, protect their reputation.*

It was getting dark when suddenly I had the urge to spend the night in my tree house. Mom had put Betsy to bed early, so I didn't have to worry about her begging to come with me. My plan was to sneak my strange little ornament out to the tree house along with a lantern from our camping gear so I could get a better look at it. I knew I would need to learn all I could about its appearance and markings before I could hope to find it in the encyclopedia.

I found both my parents in the living room sitting together on the sofa pouring over the TV Guide. I stood quietly in the doorway watching them and wondering how a day that started out so badly could end up nearly perfect. Their love and devotion for each other had never been more obvious to me. I knew at that very moment that there was nothing that the two of them could not face together. I hated to disturb their time together, but I had to get permission to sleep outside, so I reluctantly crossed the room to stand before them. Nothing else had been mentioned about the neighbors from the time we left the Catellis,' but even still, my approach was guarded. To my surprise they agreed that it was an excellent idea and even suggested I call my friend Sarah O'Malley from up the street to sleep over.

By eight o'clock Sarah and I were both seated cross-legged on the floor of the tiny tree house, my secretly acquired kerosene lantern casting a soft, warm glow around us. Staring down at the unusual gift that had been left for me by a mysterious nighttime visitor, I waited for Sarah's reaction. I had already told her about the people who moved in next door and how I'd been secretly spying on them from the porch roof, but I didn't go into detail as to what I'd seen, and I didn't tell her they were Jews. I'm not sure why.

Sarah stared at the handsomely engraved object for a long time, then picked it up and said bluntly, "Maybe it was stolen from a museum somewhere, and this guy you call 'the weird one' just stashed it here until he could find a buyer for it. And, maybe he was planning to come back for it, but you found it first. Maybe it was never intended to be a gift."

"Oh, but it most certainly was," came a voice from somewhere out in the darkness. Sarah dropped the ornament as we turned to see Ben Davis poking his head up over the ladder.

"What are you doing here?" I hissed. "Nobody said you could come up here!" *So outsiders aren't allowed in this playhouse either?* Immediately I regretted the hateful words, my heart bearing down on my conscience like a steel trap.

Ben started back down the ladder. "You're absolutely right, miss. I beg your pardon." He reached the bottom rung before looking up.

"I guess it's okay for you to come up for a few minutes, but that's all." I looked at Sarah and shrugged. Her mouth was hanging open, her eyes wide as dinner plates. "Don't you dare say a word about this to anyone,"

I warned her, just as Ben crawled through the little doorway and sat down next to me, reaching his hand out to Sarah.

"Hi, I'm Ben Davis; I live next door." He was smiling at her in the same way he had smiled at me on that first day we met at the fence. *Was I jealous?* Sarah shook his hand, still staring at me in bewilderment. I pretended not to notice. I offered him a Coke and some Little Debbies, hoping we would all relax a bit. Sarah sulked off to the corner nibbling on a Twinkie and keeping a steady gaze on Ben. There was distrust in her eyes as she glanced at me then quickly back to Ben.

After a while Ben reached for the peculiar little object still lying on the floor where Sarah had dropped it. "So, do you want to know about the menorah?"

"The what?" I looked down at what he held in his hands.

"It's a menorah," he repeated. "It's called a lamp stand in the Torah, ah ... Bible. It has been used for many thousands of years to light the way for the Hebrew people."

I looked at the little menorah. It stood about seven inches high and had six pieces coming out from the center stem, three on each side, each with a small cup attached at the top, making it a total of seven cups. *Seven lights! That's it! That's what I saw from the roof last Friday night!*"Do you burn candles in it?" I asked him.

"Yes, or sometimes olive oil; whichever we happen to have. We use it for Shabbat, and for Pesach, and other special times. You probably never heard them called that. To you it would be Sabbath and Passover." Suddenly he jumped up. "I'll be right back," he said, then dashed down the ladder and hopped the fence. This gave me the opportunity to tell Sarah about seeing the menorah in Ben's house from my front porch roof on Friday nights, and that I suspected it was him all along who I had seen leaving the tree house late on Saturday night.

"It's all very weird," I continued. "The house is all dark except for this one light, well seven lights, I guess, but all coming from this one lamp. That was before I knew they were Jews." There it was; I said it. I didn't look at her; I just waited. I didn't have to wait long.

"So it's true then, what I've heard. You are renting to Jews!" Her voice was tense. A burning began to churn in my stomach much like it did earlier in the day when I'd heard Mr. Catelli's cruel words.

"So what if we are!" I shouted. "It's our business who we rent to, Sarah! For crying out loud, what's wrong with the people in this town! Why does everyone hate Jews?"

Sarah stood to her feet, snatching up her pillow and sleeping bag. "My father says Jews are Christ killers, and it's because of them that Jesus died on the cross. You go to church, Maggie. You should know that!" She started down the ladder just as Ben returned, his hands full of tiny candles. She glared harshly at him then walked through the front gate and down the sidewalk toward her house.

"What was that all about?" Ben asked as he settled down next to me on the wooden floor. "She looked mad. Did I do something to upset her?"

"Nope, that's just Sarah." I knew I could brush this off fairly easily. "When something doesn't go her way, she runs home and pouts. She'll get over it." Still, I couldn't shake off her comment about church. *Is that what Christians believe about Jews, that they are Christ killers?* I had been in church most of my life, and I had never heard anything like that. I turned my attention back to Ben and his candles. "Whatcha got?"

"I thought you might like to see the menorah lit up—up close I mean." He grinned out of the corner of his mouth.

"You saw me? You knew I was watching you?" I was mortified! I couldn't look at him.

"Yeah, but only last week and then again this past Shabbat. We saw you climb out your window just before the sun went down and then watched to see if you would do it again, and you did. My pop thought it was cute, but Momma was afraid you were going to fall off the roof. She threatened to tell your mother, but I talked her out of it by promising her I would talk to you first. That's actually what I came to tell you at the fence yesterday, but it didn't go too well. I think I scared you off."

I glanced up at him. I was so embarrassed I couldn't speak. I had never been caught spying before and was even starting to think I was getting pretty good at it.

"I sit out on that roof all the time; I'm not gonna fall." I knew that wasn't exactly the point of the conversation, but it was the best I could do. I wasn't about to admit that I'd been spying on him and his family. After a few awkward moments I said, "Well, are you going to light it or not?"

With gentle but precise movements, Ben placed a candle in each cup, saving the middle one for last. Then he reached inside his shirt pocket and brought out another candle, slightly longer than the others. "This one is called the Shamash," he said, as he placed it in the center cup. "It is the servant candle. It is used to light all the other candles. Like this," he whispered, as he struck a match and lit the Shamash. Then carefully he lifted it out of its cup and tilted it delicately over each of the other six candles, lighting them one by one. He smiled at me as he placed the servant candle back into its proper cup. All seven little candles glowed brightly, the middle one standing just ever so slightly above the others, forming an inverted V shape.

I leaned over and blew out the lantern and stared at the menorah. From the side view the lights appeared to be blending into one larger light, just like before when I saw them the first time from the roof top. *So it wasn't my eyes playing tricks on me after all! They really do look as if they are all burning from the one light in the center—*

the servant. It was the most beautiful thing I had ever seen. For the next hour or so we talked and laughed and enjoyed each other's company, but even still, I felt that there was something strangely unsettling, lurking in the corners of my mind like a well-camouflaged rattlesnake, and I thought perhaps it had something to do with Sarah's vile accusations about the Jews.

Ben left the tree house around eleven o'clock but not before we promised to meet again next Sunday night and every Sunday night for the rest of the summer.

I learned a lot about Ben that night. I learned that he was fifteen, just two years older than I was, and that his full name in Hebrew was actually Yaakov ben David, pronounced da-veed, not David the way we say it in English. Also, he was born in Brooklyn, New York, in 1947 on Yom Kippur, but I didn't think to ask him what that was. He told me that his father fought in the war that helped establish Israel as a nation in 1948 and…that he was adopted. The man that he calls Pop was not his real father. His real father, Ari ben Yonah, died in Israel.

Ari's parents and grandparents had fled Poland in 1939 just as the Nazis were becoming a serious threat to Jews in Warsaw. They were lucky to get out when they did, he'd said. They had only been in Israel a few years when Ari met Rivkah Abram and fell in love with her. They married in 1946 just as things were starting to get really bad in Israel, known at that time as Palestine. Ben's mother soon discovered she was pregnant, and his father, fearing for her safety, made hasty provisions to send his beloved wife to America to stay with friends in New York City. Ben was born in a hospital in Brooklyn, the first in his family to be delivered by a real doctor in a real hospital. As troubles grew worse for the Jews, Ben's father wrote that he felt compelled to stay and fight for the freedom of his people. Against Rivkah's wishes, he joined an underground renegade army called the Haganah, and began building homemade bombs and bottle rockets. "Not to worry, my sweet Rivkah," he wrote, "I will join you in the states in time to see my little Yaakov take his first steps." But as the fighting continued, Ari ben Yonah never returned to his family. On May 15, 1948, just one day after Israel was declared a free state, enemies attacked the tiny nation from all directions, killing hundreds of unarmed Jews. Ari died fighting for the land and the people that he loved a few months before Ben turned a year old. Before long, Rivkah Yonah had become known as Ruby Jones and little Yaakov was just Ben. They were completely Americanized.

A few years passed, and Ruby met an older gentleman by the name of Yosef ben David (da-veed), a mutual friend of Ari's and the people that she had come to live with in New York. Yosef and his first wife, Tikvah, had been captured by the Nazis in 1941, along with their two young sons, Moshe and Aaron. They were transported to Auschwitz, a concentration camp set up to annihilate the Jewish population along with millions of other "inferiors." It was there that the four of them endured the pain of bloody needles and dull-bladed scalpels as they received their tattooed identification numbers, branding them worthless in the eyes of their enemies, and it was there that Tikvah died and their two little boys vanished. According to Ben, the boys were assumed dead by the authorities, even though there had never been any trace of them found anywhere in the camp when it was finally liberated in 1945.

Yosef spent many years searching for his children, but in the end he came to accept that they were gone, probably buried in one of the hundreds of mass graves along the roads throughout Germany. He made his way to southern France and then eventually caught a freight liner to America.

Several months after meeting Ruby, they married, and Yosef ben David became known as Joseph (Joe) Davis. A year later he legally adopted young Ben, had their names changed to the Americanized versions that everyone already knew them as, and moved his little family to Miami, Florida. When work became scarce, they ventured north, up through Georgia, landing in Tennessee. Joe was a butcher by trade and soon found work in a little kosher deli that serviced a small Jewish community. After moving around a few more times, they found our little white house and happily settled into our completely non-Jewish neighborhood. *I'm not so sure it was one of their smarter moves.*

CHAPTER SIX

I woke sometime during the night, my hair damp with dew, my knees and back aching. I had somehow managed to wiggle out of my sleeping bag and onto the bare floor. I decided I'd had enough outdoor adventure for one night and climbed down the ladder.

Back inside my house, I gently tiptoed across the kitchen floor to the stairs, glancing at the clock over the stove: 4:20 AM. *I won't have long to sleep*, I realized as I started up the stairs to my room, carefully avoiding the squeaky seventh step that never failed to alert my sister of my coming and going. I knew if she heard me, she would immediately cry out for Mom and there would be no end to the barrage of questions as to why I was up at this hour, and where was Sarah? My bed felt warm and soft, and as I tucked my little treasured menorah securely under my pillow, I faded off to sleep.

Help me! They're coming! Who are you? What do you want? Help me, please! Who are you? What is this place? Who's coming? Who? They're coming! Don't let them take me, Maggie, please! Look at me, boy. Let me see your face. Who are you? I am Moshe. It's too late. Too late. Too la—

I bolted upright, slinging my covers onto the floor. *Where are you?* I looked around the dark room, staring for a minute at Betsy, snuggled safely with her baby doll, sleeping soundly. My face and hands were hot with sweat, my mouth parched. *Was it real? Was it a dream? Who is Moshe?* Then I remembered Ben's story about his stepfather's two boys who disappeared during the Holocaust. *Was he calling to me from somewhere beyond reality? No, no,* I reasoned with myself. *That doesn't happen. It was just a dream, a really bad dream.* I instinctively reached under my pillow and felt for the menorah. *It's still there,* and although knowing that brought me some measure of comfort, I couldn't shake the uncontrollable feeling in my gut that something wasn't right. I lay awake watching through the little clerestory window as the sky lightened into morning.

Mom was already up with coffee made for my dad and getting her first load of wash onto the line. I fixed myself a bowl of cornflakes and retreated to the living room to watch cartoons with Betsy. I'd noticed that my father was not in his usual chair at the kitchen table with his newspaper but thought it best not to ask why. I finished my cereal, took the bowl to the sink and rinsed out the remaining milk and sugar. Mom was coming through the back door with an empty laundry basket. *She's going to have me doing laundry all day*, I thought, *while precious sits on her hind quarters eating Little Debbie and making messes for me to clean up*. It was obvious that the lack of sleep was working its spell in my brain, making me tired and grumpy. But instead of handing me the basket, she smiled at me and headed upstairs to gather up the dirty clothes from my room. *Well, that was different. Maybe she's finally going to give me that break I've been harping about all summer*. I dried the bowl and spoon and put everything away in the proper cabinet then stole a quick glance out of the kitchen window.

Mrs. Davis was hanging wet laundry on her clothesline as well. *Gee, I wonder if she and Mom spoke to each other. What a shame they will probably never get to be friends like Ben and me.* And even though I never got around to telling Ben about all the mess that was going on, I was sure that nothing could spoil our newly found friendship. I smiled as I recalled his cute grin and felt my cheeks flush. I glanced out the window again. Ruby Davis—Rivkah—truly was a beautiful woman, even with her hair tied back and covered with a bandana. She was slender and graceful, even standing at an ordinary clothesline wearing an ordinary house dress on an ordinary Monday morning. Looking closer I noticed that she had the exact same complexion color as Ben, a creamy darkness, smooth as silk.

Suddenly my mother appeared in the kitchen, the laundry basket piled high with sheets and pillow cases, with one little obscure tree-shaped shiny object lying on top of the pile. I swallowed hard. She set the basket on the table and walked out of the room taking the menorah with her. "Mom, wait ... I can explain ..."

"Save it!" The tone in her voice was unmistakable. This was a matter to be turned over to my father. I went to sit on the front porch swing in the bright morning sunlight, anticipating my condemned fate.

I was stunned to see my dad coming down the sidewalk from the direction of Sarah O'Malley's house. He was walking faster than usual and seemed taller; his shoulders squared off instead of casually hunched forward like they were normally. He looked determined. I was sure it had something to do with last night. I jumped off the swing and ran upstairs to my room and closed the door. Should I pray? I could climb out onto the roof, wait until he goes through the front door, then jump down and run. *You can't run if you break your leg, stupid!* Or I could just sit here on the side of my bed and wait.

CHAPTER SEVEN

"Mary Margaret Sanders, you get down here this instant!" He used my full name, something I had only heard him do once before when I was seven years old and stole a Hershey bar from the five and dime.

I left the sanctity of my little room and started down the stairs, not even bothering to avoid the seventh step. I followed the sound of my mother's pitiful sobs, finding them both seated at the big dining room table, the menorah on the table in plain sight. Neither of them looked at me when I walked into the room; they just sat staring at the menorah.

I stood there before them feeling like a condemned criminal facing life without parole, waiting to hear my inevitable sentencing to eternal damnation when suddenly the phone rang. We all jumped. I hurried to the living room to answer it.

"Hello ...yes, sir, he is ...yes, sir, one minute please." I called out to my father. "It's for you, Dad," I tried to keep my voice steady and unpretentious. He reached for the receiver without looking at me. This was hard; he was really mad this time. My father had had to discipline me in the past on many occasions, but his heart toward me had never changed. Mom's way of dealing with me was not so. She would get all mushy, crying like a baby and swearing that if I truly loved her, I would never do such a thing (like steal a candy bar), so apparently I didn't love her anymore, and I would, of course, be guilty as charged. I honestly don't know which was worse to deal with, but I was leaning more and more in favor of the mush. Having your own father treat you like you were being excommunicated from the family was the worst kind of emotional pain.

I returned to the dining room and took an empty seat. Mom turned her head slightly, looked at me from the corner of her eye, and then burst into tears, turning back around completely.

"Mom, please don't cry," I attempted to comfort her, thinking that maybe if things got really bad here in the next few minutes, she might return the favor. "I know I messed up really bad and Dad is sore at me, but it's not like I killed anybody! I was just being neighborly like you always taught me to do." *That's right; twist it around so it's her fault; that should fix things.* She turned around to look at me and then cried all the more.

At that moment my father entered the room, looking pale and worn down. I lowered my eyes only to find myself staring at the menorah. Biting my bottom lip, I slowly looked back up at my dad. He was tired, I could tell, and greatly disturbed. But there was more, something I did not recall ever seeing on his face. It was the look of defeat, like he had just lost at something he really needed to win. He slumped into the end chair, folding his arms on the table and resting his head on them.

Mom got up and went to him. "Ted, we can deal with this later; this is enough for now. Come out to the kitchen and get your coffee. Come on, honey. You're going to be late for work." He didn't move. She tried again. "Ted, Maggie is sorry for all this mess; I just know she is, and I don't see where punishing her any more is going to fix anything, so let's just forget about it." Suddenly she grabbed the menorah. "Here, I'll just throw this thing into the trash and that will be the end of that." She started toward the kitchen, menorah in hand.

I jumped up and lunged at her. "No! You can't do that! It's mine!" I don't know how my father got from where he was to where I was so fast, but before my hands ever touched the menorah, his hands touched me, his strong arms wrapping around me like a straight jacket. I didn't want to fight, but it wasn't fair, and in my heart I knew that what they were doing was wrong. I pushed hard against my father and tried again to grab the precious lamp from my mother. She gasped and ran to the kitchen. "No, Mommy! No! Don't throw it away! Please!" I screamed, pleading with everything that was in me.

Then, right there in the dining room with my father's arms wound tightly around me, I prayed for the first time in my life, for something I desperately needed. "Father God, please help me!" I screamed. "Show them that the menorah can't hurt them and that I love them with all my heart. Make them see that I never meant to hurt them, and let everything be okay. Please, God, help me!"

My father released his grip, his arms falling instantly to his sides. I was crying uncontrollably now, my shoulders heaving with every painful sob. My legs wobbled; I was sure I was about to faint as I dropped into the chair, unable to hold back the tears.

My mother moved slowly back into the room, the shiny little menorah still in her hand. With trembling fingers, she carefully lowered it to the table in front of me. Then with the gentle words of a loving mother she spoke. "You're right, Maggie; it is yours. Go put it away now, and we will talk later."

That was it. Dad didn't protest, so I quickly snatched the menorah and ran to my room. Betsy was on her bed, brushing her doll's hair.

"What's happening, Maggie?" Her voice trembled with fear. "Why were you screaming so loud?" Tears welled up in her eyes, spilling down her cheeks like tiny rivers of misery. I reached out to her, and she ran into my arms, dropping her doll at my feet.

"Shush now, sissy. It's okay." We sat holding each other for a long time, our tears mingled and flowing freely now. I knew that eventually we would all have to talk, get this out in the open, but I prayed that it would not be today. This was enough heartache for one day.

Chapter Eight

Things were still tense when my mother called Betsy and me to come downstairs for lunch. We ate our meal in silence, no one daring to make eye contact. Even my sister, who had no idea what had transpired earlier that morning, as she had given up the cartoons in favor of her dolls before all hell broke loose, sat respectfully quiet, munching her chips and picking at the crust on her tuna sandwich.

I didn't want to eat, the knot in my stomach feeling more like tangled barbed wire; but I wasn't about to do anything to create more stress on my parents or undesired consequences for myself, so I picked up my sandwich and took a nibble. It was my dad who spoke first.

"I'm not going to go into all the details at this time, but I think you all should know that I have been temporarily suspended from my position at the plant."

Glancing at Betsy, he continued. "I really don't want to discuss the reasons right now, but I will say that unless things change, and I think you all know what I am referring to, this could lead to more permanent actions." He took a gulp of coffee, glaring at me as he replaced the cup back in its saucer. I held the bite of tuna fish in my mouth, too scared to swallow, respectfully lowering my eyes.

"That was Mr. Catelli who called this morning, telling me not to bother coming in today, or the rest of the week. He seems to think that a week off without pay will help clear my head so I can think straighter." I could tell from the hint of sarcasm in his voice that it was already more serious than just a temporary layoff. He took another swig of coffee. "I'm assuming that Mr. O'Malley may have had something to do with that, since he is an important member of the board of directors over the plant. He also called early this morning before any of you were out of bed, asking me to join him for coffee on his patio." He stopped talking long enough to give me another long, hard stare.

Mom reached across the table and touched his arm. "Ted, you promised…let us try to have a pleasant afternoon, and then maybe later this evening we can discuss with Maggie what you and Mr. O'Malley talked about." He finished his lunch in silence. I asked to be excused from the table, leaving a half-eaten sandwich and handful of chips on my plate. Picking up my glass of iced tea, I retreated to the solidarity of my tree house.

I didn't see any sign of Ben or his parents and couldn't help wonder if they already knew somehow of the turmoil in the neighborhood. *Maybe God has a way of protecting them from people like us,* I thought miserably. When it came right down to it, I knew in my heart that I would rather see the Davis family leave town and risk never seeing Ben again than for my dad to lose his job at the plant. It felt selfish and hypocritical, but I didn't care. I loved my family, crazy as they were at times, and I didn't want anything coming along that might threatened to change things. The truth is, I'm not so sure that I was all that much different from Mr. Catelli, or Mr. O'Malley, or Sarah, or my father. I just wanted peace in the world, and it needed to start right here on my street.

So that's it; the Jews had to go. It was the only way. I sipped on my glass of sweet iced tea, feeling smug and satisfied that I had come to this conclusion. *Besides,* I reasoned, *they are only one family, and the rest of us outnumber them—majority rules.*

I heard clanking below and knew it must be Betsy, coming to annoy me with her bundle of mismatched trinkets and toys with missing parts. "What do you want?" I snapped at her as she stuck her head into the doorway of the tree house. "You know you're not allowed up here unless I say so."

"I brought you something," she answered timidly. "Can I come in?"

"Okay, but you're not staying all day. I need to be alone to think." She climbed in, dragging her Mickey Mouse book satchel behind her. *Great! All I need is a bunch of Barbie dolls scattered all over the place!* After settling on the old cushion, she unbuckled her satchel, partially emptying its contents into the middle of the floor, obviously planning to stay longer than allowed: there were two Curious George books, three shirtless Barbies, a half eaten box of Cracker Jacks, and a handful of marbles.

"Look Betsy, this is enough junk for you to play with. Leave the rest. ..."

"I got it," she exclaimed excitedly, as she pulled the menorah out of the satchel. Proudly, she placed it in the center of the floor between the two of us. My heart fluttered as I caught my breath.

"What are you doing with that?" How did you get it?" I hadn't meant to startle her, but I was already in so much trouble over that thing, and I didn't want Mom and Dad thinking that I was dragging Betsy into something. "You take this right back inside and put it back where you got it. I don't ever want to see you with it again, do you understand me?" What was I saying? Betsy's lips began to tremble. Was I telling my own little sister that there was something wrong with the menorah? Something fearful and evil? I picked up the little lamp stand. It was polished but old and scratched, a dent in one corner of the base. I hadn't really looked at it closely until now. There were writings of some sort on the extended branches and even more down the center. What did they mean? Was it worth risking my own reputation and that of my family's to find out? I didn't have an answer, and I didn't know just yet what

I was going to do about this peculiar object, but I knew I couldn't disregard it as so many people had done in the past. Yes, I was selfish and self-righteous at times, even most of the time—but full of hate and prejudice? Arrogance and conceit? I don't know; I hoped not. I picked up the Cracker Jacks and shook the box to loosen the stale popcorn. I dumped a few kernels into my hand and then offered some to Betsy. She smiled, her tear-dampened eyes shimmering with joy at my meager gesture, and stuck out her hands, waiting for me to fill them. *It probably wouldn't hurt to be a little nicer,* I reminded myself as I picked a piece of sticky caramel corn out of my back tooth.

CHAPTER NINE

The conversation that evening between my parents and me went slightly better than I had anticipated, probably because no one wanted a repeat of the morning fiasco. My father was even lighthearted as he played with Betsy and her pick-up-sticks. I sat quietly, feigning interest in the game, all the while contemplating an answer to the inevitable question: What was Ben Davis doing in the tree house last night after dark? At long last, Dad set Betsy aside on the footstool and looked at me.

"Maggie, I know you think that your mother and I are the most unreasonable people in the world, but you are going to have to trust me when I say that we have your best interest at heart." He looked over at my mom for support. She had picked up her knitting basket and was busy working on a pair of socks for Betsy.

I think she pretended not to hear him. He tried again. "You see, Maggie, your mother and I believe that it is best if people of like mind and faith stick together, not because they think they are better than anyone else, but, well, it just works out better, that's all." He looked uncomfortable as if he knew what I was thinking— *Weak argument.*

I wasn't sure it was my turn to speak, but I decided to try anyway. "Dad, I'm really sorry about this morning. I don't know what got into me. I guess I was—"

"That's not what this is about, Maggie," he interrupted. "We have moved on past that. This is about you and that kid next door becoming friends. You have to get it through your head, Mary Margaret, this is about our future in this town, your future—yours and Betsy's. If somebody who is over me says something has to be a certain way, then like it or not, that's the way it's got to be. There's no arguing the matter." He stood up and began pacing around the room. Mom looked up from her knitting. She was like a mountain lion guarding her cub from a Kodiak. Her little bifocals resting on the end of her nose made her look matronly.

She watched him pace for a few minutes and then went back to her basket of yarn.

"Dad, the only reason I was nice to Ben Davis is because you and Mom had told me when they first moved in to go over and say hello, but I didn't. I felt bad about it; that's all. It's not like I was planning to marry the guy!"

Dad spun around to face me. Mom lay her knitting aside. "So you were getting friendly with the Jewish kid, huh! Maybe you better tell me why it took Mr. O'Malley to inform me that Ben Davis was in the tree house at ten o'clock last night with two thirteen-year-old girls while your mother and I lay sleeping in our bed, completely unaware? Let's hear it, Mary Margaret, and don't put your cute little spin on it either. Tell the truth!"

Mom rose to her feet. "Not until you sit down, Ted. You said you weren't going to lose your temper, and I'm afraid that is exactly what is about to happen. If you want her to talk, you will have to sit down." Dad sat back down in his chair.

Betsy went to sit with Mom. "Sweetie, why don't you and I go find some cookies out in the kitchen, and then you can take them upstairs for a bedtime snack, okay?" They disappeared into the kitchen leaving me with the Kodiak. I braced myself for round two.

"All right, Maggie," my father said with a little more composure. "Start at the beginning and tell me everything." He waited. I wasn't exactly sure what his definition of everything was, but I decided it wouldn't help matters for him to know that I'd been sitting on the porch roof spying on the neighbors, so I started with the encounter Betsy and I had with Ben at the fence. I tried hard to think of everything that was important to the subject without being self-incriminating. But I knew better than to paint myself too saintly as well because my parents knew perfectly well what kind of kid they had on their hands. I finished my story by telling him about the beauty of the menorah and how it looked so small and innocent yet powerful enough to light the way for the Jewish people for thousands of years, borrowing from Ben's words, of course.

My mother had rejoined us just as I was telling about the candles and the Shamash and what it meant. She seemed genuinely interested, but my father wasn't going to let all this pretty talk sway his decision. He had already predetermined his judgment, based on the former threats of his employer. As he laid down the law, I felt my whole world shrink down to the size of a golf ball: grounded for the remainder of the summer with the exception of family outings, no sleepovers in the tree house ever again, no hanging out with Ben, and most of all, I was never to speak of this to anyone, ever.

CHAPTER TEN

The first part of the week was stifling, and not just the weather, although I did hear the weatherman on the six o'clock news say the temperature in the Tennessee Valley was expected to reach into the upper nineties by mid to late August. *He wasn't lying,* I thought to myself as I mopped the sweat beads from my forehead. I tried not to look in the direction of the little white house as I removed the last of the warm, sun-dried bed linens from the clothesline.

I had been staying to myself for the most part, only venturing out into the backyard to help with the laundry, not even daring to think about spending any time alone in my tree house. *Thinking about stuff just seems to get me into more trouble anyway,* I reasoned. *It's probably for the best that I just stay busy.* Besides, with Dad laid off all week and watching me like a hawk watches a field rat, there wasn't much opportunity for me to study my menorah or keep an eye out for Ben. I muddled through my daily chores, picking up after Betsy and trying to be helpful to my mother. I had nothing to look forward to, so, in my opinion, there was no need for smiling. I guess Mom must have noticed because by Thursday morning, things took a turn for the better. To my surprise she had come up with a relatively good idea. "We should pack a picnic and go to the river for lunch." The day was perfect, already full of sunshine and high temperatures; plus we hadn't been swimming all summer.

It didn't take long to load up the station wagon with inner tubes and beach towels; Mom got the food together, and Betsy stuffed every Barbie she could find into her book satchel with her flip-flops and her Daisy Duck sunglasses. In less than one hour, we were sitting on the banks of our favorite swimming hole along the Tennessee River, ready for a day of fun in the sun. Several families and small groups of older teenagers were gathered close by to enjoy the day as well, and for the first time in two weeks, my family relaxed. It was almost too good to be true.

I was about twenty yards from the river bank, floating around on my inner tube when I spotted a familiar dark-haired kid swimming toward me. *Oh no!* I began paddling my float as hard as I could to get back to shore before he reached me. Suddenly he disappeared under water. I looked over my left shoulder and spotted my dad playing in the water with Betsy. Mom was spreading lunch out on the blanket. Then out of the blue I felt something brush against my leg. I jerked my knee up out of the water, suppressing a scream. Ben poked his head up from the water, grinning from ear to ear.

"Hey, kid! Where ya been?" Splashing water in my face, he ducked under again, coming up on the opposite side, directly in view of my father.

"Ben Davis," I snapped, "what on earth are you doing here?"

"Hey, crab apple, it's a public swimming hole last time I looked," he teased. He swam around to face me square on. Seeing that I was not amused, he lowering his brow as he questioned me, "Is there some reason I wouldn't want to swim here, Maggie?"

I tried to ignore the question. *If my father sees me talking to him, it will be all over! He will think I somehow planned this little rendezvous, and I will be in the worst kind of serious trouble!* Ben was treading water in front of me, waiting for an answer.

"Maggie, Ted, Betsy, lunch is ready!" Mom was standing on the bank, looking right in my direction.

"I can't be seen with you, not now—not ever! My dad said so!" I tried to sound stern and condescending, hoping it would send him on his way.

"You're kidding me, right? He didn't really say we can't hang out, did he?" I nodded nervously, checking the riverbank. Dad and Betsy were drying off as Mom fixed plates of hot dogs, potato salad and deviled eggs.

"I have to go, Ben. Please don't ask me any more questions. If it's safe, I'll send a signal tonight for you to meet me at the tree house; three flashes of light from the porch roof. I gotta go!" I paddled away from Ben toward the bank, praying that Betsy and my parents hadn't seen him.

As I grabbed a towel from the back of the station wagon, I stole a glance across the river to where I had met up with Ben, but he was gone. Mom handed me a plate and I settled down on the blanket to enjoy my lunch. So far, so good.

The picnic was fun, reminding me of the good times we'd had and the closeness we'd felt for each other before the trouble started over our new neighbors. I took a bite of my hot dog: mustard and sweet pickle relish, just the way I liked it. I looked up at my mother and smiled. She was like most moms I guess, kind and sweet-natured, eager to do for her family. She learned from her mother the way to a man's heart and managed to keep my father happy. She seemed afraid of confrontation at any level; nothing to her was worth a fight, except perhaps if her children were threatened. She didn't seem especially angry about the Davises living next door, but if my father told her to never speak to them, she would never speak to them and would probably never ask why. If anything, I think she couldn't care less who lived there as long as they kept the grass cut and didn't throw rocks at her kids.

My father was loyal and good at heart, willing to stop at nothing to do the right thing, but not always so clear on what that right thing was. I believed with all my heart that if he would just get to know the Davis family, he would see that they were just like everybody else—hard-working, sociable, trustworthy, honest, and just as God-fearing as the next guy. So what was stopping him? The only thing that I had ever known to stop my father from going ahead with something was fear—fear that someone in his family would get hurt. Could he be motivated by that same kind of fear now? But why? What was the driving force behind his fear of the Davises? I had a hard time believing that my dad was a bigot, a racist, in spite of some of the things he had been saying lately. No, it was something big, something he kept bottled up inside his soul that was making him feel the need to rid the neighborhood of the Jews. I had to find out, and soon.

It was getting late and time to leave the peaceful river bank. I helped my dad pack up the car, feeling differently toward him somehow, to the point that I couldn't resist stopping to give him a hug.

"What was that for?" he asked in surprise.

"I just wanted to say thanks for a great day, Dad," I replied, and then pulled away quickly before he saw the tears welling up in my eyes. How would I ever explain a sudden burst of tears on a day like this? I turned around to grab the rest of the damp towels and threw them into the back of the station wagon. As we pulled out onto the pavement, an old dark grey Ford sedan passed slowly by. I looked up just in time to see Joe Davis waving at my father, my dad looking away, not returning the friendly gesture.

CHAPTER ELEVEN

I didn't want to deceive my parents by sneaking around to see Ben, but I wasn't confident that I could ask permission and have it granted. I was grounded after all, and not seeing Ben was part of that. I also knew that if I got caught, it would only get worse. I had to make a decision. After a good half hour of sitting there on the damp, slippery shingles of the porch roof, I clicked on my flashlight; then off; then on and off two more times. Then I waited for a response. *There it was!* Three flashes of light coming from Ben's front porch. *He must have been sitting there all along waiting for me to signal him.* I hurried back inside to get my sweater and the bag of cookies I had smuggled from the kitchen after dinner. Slipping the menorah under my sweater, I tiptoed quietly down the stairs, ever mindful of the squeaky seventh step, and out the back door. It was already close to midnight, but I had to be sure everyone in the house was asleep before venturing out. Ben was waiting for me at the tree house.

"Long time, no see." He grinned as he did the ladies first gesture, indicating that I should go ahead of him up the ladder. He was carrying a bag as well, and I was hoping it was some Coke or Kool-Aid because I had forgotten to pack anything for us to drink. I took a seat on the boat cushion; Ben sat down cross-legged on my sleeping bag. I slipped the menorah from under my sweater as he was fishing around in his bag. "I hope you like grape soda," he said with a shyness I hadn't detected before. It was kind of cute. "It's all I could find on such short notice."

I knew he was teasing me, and after my nasty remarks at the lake earlier, I was genuinely relieved that he wanted to talk to me at all. I took the bottle of pop and then looked at the cap. "How am I supposed to. . . ." He handed me the bottle opener from his shirt pocket. I smiled and thanked him. "All I brought was some oatmeal cookies," I said apologetically.

He accepted the cookie graciously and took a bite. "These are fantastic! Did you make them?"

"No, my mom is the chief cook at my house; I'm just the bottle washer." He laughed lightheartedly as he enjoyed his snack.

We didn't talk for a while, just eating our cookies and drinking our grape Nehis and looking around as if to say, "This is nice, no grownups, no little kids, no nosey neighbors; just us."

Curiosity finally got the best of me, and I had to ask, "So, what else do you have in your bag?" I was sure he hadn't lugged that big book bag all the way over here just for two soda pops; he could have carried those in his hands.

With a hint of excitement in his voice, he reached into his bag and found a small, white cloth with lace edging and spread it out on the floor between us. "Well, there are matches to light the menorah, and candles too, of course, and, let's see, I have a necklace to show you, and one other thing; here it is; it's called a *tzitzit*. I'll tell you all about it for another one of those cookies."

I was spellbound as Ben laid out all his treasures at my feet. So many cool and interesting things in his life, and all I could come up with was a bag of cookies. "I want to know everything about you," I gushed without thinking. I felt the heat rising in my face and was thankful that it was dark, and we hadn't lit the menorah yet.

Ben laughed again, his playful mood becoming contagious. "And I want to know how your mom made these cookies. I do a lot of the cooking at my house in the summer because my folks spend most of their time either at work in the deli or at the synagogue teaching kids Hebrew. You will have to tell her I want her recipe."

"That's not possible, remember? I'm not supposed to have anything to do with you." I knew he deserved an explanation, but I hated to have to tell him the truth for fear he would regret giving me the beautiful menorah. But for some reason, I found myself telling him anyway. "My mom found the menorah in my room, and my dad hit the ceiling, and so now my life is over for the rest of the summer." Taking another swig of my Nehi, I closed my eyes tight, pressing my tears into submission.

"Man, I am so sorry, Maggie! I had no idea they were like that, I mean, when your dad rented us the house, we were hoping to get to know all of you and maybe make some new friends." He was obviously disappointed over our situation, but not all that surprised. "Don't worry about it, Maggie," he said wryly, "persecution and anti-Semitism is nothing new to the Jews."

Blinking away the tears, I looked down at the little display of Ben's personal belongings. *If he is this eager to share his faith and personal history with me, why would he have been any different with my father?* It was becoming clear to me that he and his family had not intended to trick my father at all.

I studied the display for a moment and then gently reached down and picked up the candles, placing them in each of the cups, remembering to put the tallest candle in the center. Ben struck a match and lit our menorah, warming our hearts as we smiled at each other. Then he picked up the knotted blue and white strings he had referred to as tzitzit and gave them to me. I handled them gently, almost reverently, rolling the delicate threads around in my fingers as I studied the hard little knots. *What could all this mean?*

As if reading my mind, Ben began explaining in a soft whisper. "The Torah, what you call the Old Testament, tells us that we are to make fringes and put them on the four corners of our garments, so that when we look at them, we will be reminded to obey the Commandments. The blue thread, called a *tekehlet* in Hebrew, is twisted into each of the four fringes. I don't know for sure if using blue thread is an actual commandment or not, and some people use other colors, but personally, I prefer the blue; so does my pop." He hadn't taken his eyes off the blue and white threads, and I could tell that whatever they meant, it was something very important to him. I sat quietly, hoping he would tell me more. "My people have been doing this for thousands of years," he continued. "I'm not even sure they fully understand what it all means, but they do it anyway, out of obedience."

Ben laid the tzitzit back on the cloth, the light from the menorah shimmering against his handsome young face. Then slowly he took off his jacket and draped it over his head and lifted his hands to about waist high, his palms turned up. Not knowing what else to do, I followed his example, using my sweater for a head covering. He closed his eyes for a minute and then began to speak in Hebrew: "*Baruah atah Adonai Elohainu Melech Haolam, asher Kiddisshanu b'mitzotav v'tzivanu la'asot tzitzit."* He opened his eyes and smiled at me as he spoke. "It means, "Blessed are you, Lord our God, King of the universe, who sanctified us with your commandments, and commanded us to make the tzitzit."

I was awestruck. He seemed to me to be the smartest, most honest human being on the face of the earth, and here he was sitting on the floor of my tree house. I was speechless.

We finished our snack and then Ben began gathering up his belongings, carefully placing them inside his bag; all except the necklace. It still lay on the white cloth where he had first put it earlier, untouched. He looked at me and winked. "Oh, I almost forgot...this is for you. It is called a *chai*, hard to say if you weren't brought up Jewish." He chuckled. "It means 'life' in Hebrew. We say *L'Chaim*—to life! I hope you like it." He handed me the little silver charm dangling from a delicate chain. Accepting the generous gift, I fastened it securely around my neck and smiled at Ben.

Ben smiled back, looking pleased. Then his smile faded slightly. "I don't want you to get into any more trouble, so you might want to tuck it inside your shirt."

"Good idea," I replied, sliding the charm inside of my blouse. It felt cold against my skin but warm at the same time. "I'll wear it forever," I promised. I stood to my feet and stretched. "It's getting late. I guess you better go and I better get back inside. I'll let you know when we can meet again." I blew out the candles on the menorah, and Ben carefully lifted them out of the cup holders and placed them in his bag.

"I had a great evening, Ben," I whispered. "I hope it won't be too long before we can do this again."

"Yeah, me too." He started toward the ladder then stopped. Looking at me with a hint of sadness in his smile, he said, "Maggie, I just want you to know that you are the best friend I have ever had," and with that, he was down the ladder and over the fence in a flash.

I climbed down slowly, wondering where all this would lead me. Ben was fast becoming my best friend, yet my parents forbade me to see him. Standing in the damp grass, I gazed through the darkness at the little white house next door. "I hope you never have to leave me, Ben Davis," I whispered. I turned my eyes upward to the heavens and prayed, "Lord, please help me find a way to fix this mess I'm in with my parents, so maybe they will come to know Ben and love him the way I do. Amen."

Love; I hadn't thought much about that, outside my own little immediate family, but here it was, living right next door. As I quietly dressed for bed, instinctively my fingers went to my throat, where the little silver charm had found a new home. *Life, very appropriate,* I thought as I snuggled down into the warmth of my bed. *Life must surely be precious to a people who have been hated and persecuted as much as the Jews.*

Chapter Twelve

"Mr. Catelli has invited us up to Lake Sharon this coming Saturday to spend the day with him and his family," my father was saying to my mom as I came downstairs. *Oh no! Please don't say we're going! Please!* "And I think it would be a good idea if we went. If he is making a genuinely friendly gesture, the least we can do is comply. Anyway, it won't kill us to go." I looked at my mother for reassurance that this was indeed not a good idea.

"That's a fine idea, Ted." She smiled her sweetest smile and glanced in my direction. "Don't you think so, Maggie?"

I reached for a bowl and scooped out a glob of oatmeal from the pot on the stove, looking at my mother in disbelief. *After what that man did to your husband, you think it's a good idea to go spend a whole day at the lake with the likes of him and his family? That's insane!* I grabbed a slice of cinnamon toast from the plate on the back of the stove and sat down at the table. *You'd think there was enough crazy in this world that my parents would not feel the need to create more!* I looked up from my bowl; they were both staring at me, waiting.

"Sure, I guess so." I swallowed a spoonful of the sticky, hot cereal. Mom handed me a glass of cold milk to wash it down, but it was more than just oatmeal caught in my throat. I knew I had to find a way to get out of this. "But couldn't I just stay home this time? I've wanted to rearrange my room, and that would be a good time to get it done." *Lame excuse!* I couldn't care less about which way my bed was turned or on what wall the dresser sat. They looked puzzled.

"Maggie, it's a long way up to the lake, and we probably won't be back before dark," Mom said. "I would feel better if you went with us. Besides, you girls love going fishing and diving off the dock. Remember when you and your daddy caught that big-mouth bass and it nearly pulled you out of the boat? You don't want to miss out on a fun trip now, do you, honey?" She handed me another piece of toast, looking at me with beseeching eyes. "This will probably be our last summer out-ing before school starts back in a few weeks and fall weather sets in. I'm sure you and Betsy will have a good time."

So it's settled, then. I wonder why they bother asking my opinion if they have already decided the matter? I finished my breakfast in silence and went back upstairs to get dressed.

Three days later, on a warm and lovely Saturday morning, we were sitting on the banks of Lake Sharon, nestled in the hills of northwest Tennessee, a beautiful area known as the Land Between the Lakes. The smell of campfire and pinecones lay heavy in the air, and I noticed that some of the elm trees were already starting to change color. If I let it, this beauty that I was surrounded with could easily lighten my mood and give me a sense of happiness and well-being, but instead I was miserable, not only because I was being forced to spend this glorious day with people I despised, but because I hadn't seen Ben since our last meeting in the tree house, and I missed him terribly. The last thing I wanted to do was hang out all day with Maria Catelli.

I had my swimsuit on under my shorts and halter top but I wasn't sure I wanted to get in the water, so there was no need in peeling out of my clothes just yet. My mother was quite modest and never wore a swimsuit to my knowledge. She occasionally wore a pair of slacks if we were doing something that a skirt was simply out of the question, but I never knew her to show much skin. Today she wore dungarees rolled up to just below her knees and a sleeveless blouse tied at the waist. She looked younger than I was used to seeing her and cute somehow. My dad had shown his approval by giving her a little hug and kiss just as we were leaving the house earlier this morning. It was odd to see him displaying his affections toward her in front of us kids, so I had turned away. I knew I was just being stubborn by allowing myself to feel annoyed at everything.

Mr. Catelli and my father were down at the dock putting Mr. Catelli's boat into the water. They would drive back up to the camping area to get us when they were ready to go out on the lake. Being in the big cabin cruiser would be fun, I had to admit, and if I could manage to avoid Maria and her little brother long enough, this might even turn out to be a better trip than I had anticipated.

I was glad that Betsy got along well with the Catelli's young son, William, and even though he was only a year younger than she was, she smothered him with a childlike motherly affection that he seemed to enjoy, so they played well together. The obvious side effect to that was that she stayed out of my hair for the most part.

We spent the better half of the day in the boat, fishing and sunbathing. Mom and Mrs. Catelli fixed lunch from a picnic basket prepared ahead of time by Mrs. Jacobsen, the Catellis' cook. We had turkey and Swiss cheese sandwiches, pastrami on rye with fancy brown mustard, macaroni salad, all kinds of homemade pickles, olives, and slices of cucumbers and tomatoes. We drank Southern style sweet tea and sodas, and after all that, Mrs. Catelli brought out a huge four-layer chocolate cake. It was an end-of-the-summer feast to be sure, quickly replacing the frown on my face with an approving smile.

"If we had a cook like Mrs. Jacobsen, we would have to take her everywhere we went," my mother said, complimenting the Catelli chef. "My, what a wonderful meal, didn't you think so, Ted?" Taking another big bite of cake, he rubbed his stomach in grand approval.

"Mrs. Jacobsen doesn't work on Saturday, or we would have included her, of course," Mrs. Catelli explained. "From the beginning when we first hired her, she was adamant about having Saturday off, but she always prepares something for us the day before and then insists that we leave the dishes for her to clean up when she returns on Sunday morning."

"She's a strange old bird, that's for sure," Mr. Catelli chimed in. "Why, sometimes she will even show up late Saturday night just to see if there are any dishes that need to be washed or laundry needing done. All in all, we're real pleased with the ol' gal."

After lunch Maria offered to entertain my sister and me in her cabin below deck, and although I was reluctant to oblige, my own curiosity got the upper hand. I soon found myself seated on the bottom bunk of the children's quarters of the massive cruiser, wondering why this sudden change of heart. It didn't take long to discover what was on her mind.

"My father says you still have those Jews living next door to you, and I think it's just horrible how you have let them move in like that," she blurted out as soon as she had securely closed the door to the cabin. "Before you know it, Maggie Sanders, they will take over that whole neighborhood! The very idea of even wanting to be friends with one of them! You ought to know better than that, Maggie! My father says Jews ruin everything! He says they are dirty and spread disease among the clean folks. And, if they don't leave, it won't be long until all the kids in your neighborhood come down with some dreadful sickness."

She was just as evil and vile as her father, and I was fast losing my temper. I clenched my fists and tried to keep my voice low and even.

"You don't know what you're talking about, Maria! You don't even know these people! How dare you speak such terrible things about them!" My face was hot with fury, my hands trembling in anger at her vicious accusations. I continued my onslaught, my heart pounding with every word that flew out of my mouth. "You are nothing but a spoiled, rotten brat, and I don't care if you tell on me for saying it because it's true! And I don't care what your daddy says about the Davises because he's a liar and doesn't know what he's talking about either. If you'd ever met Ben Davis, you would take back everything you ever said about Jews! Why, I'll bet you don't even know any Jewish people! I'll even bet you wouldn't know a Jew if one jumped up and bit you on your big, fat Italian nose!" I grabbed my sister's hand and pulled her to her feet. "Come on, Betsy. We're going back up with Mom and Dad. We aren't staying here a minute longer!" I reached for the doorknob just as Maria grasped my arm.

"Wait, Maggie," she pleaded. "I'm sorry." I pulled away from her and opened the cabin door. "Don't leave, Maggie, please. I promised my mother I would be nice to you today, and if you go I'll be in big trouble. I said I was sorry, didn't I?"

My gut told me to leave anyway, but for some reason I backed away from the door and sat back down on the edge of the bunk. What good would it do to cause a scene out here in the middle of the lake anyway? It's not as though anything could be done to resolve this right now. *I might as well wait until I get home and hopefully talk to Ben. He is the only person I can trust to talk to me without going nuts.*

Maria began speaking more softly now as if she was truly sorry for her cruel words. "I really didn't mean what I said about the Davis family, Maggie. I don't know anything about those people or any other Jews for that matter. I only know what my father says about Jews and Negros and foreigners! He hates them all, and I have no idea why but especially Jews." She collapsed across the bunk bed in tears.

I was still mad at her for what she'd said, but now that she was crying, I had to do something. I sat down next to her and motioned for Betsy to get the box of tissues from Maria's nightstand and bring them to me. Handing her the tissues, I said, "Okay, look, it's not that bad. I forgive you for saying what you did. I get mad and say stupid stuff too, so it's over." Maria sat up and blew her nose. "Just promise me you won't ever say things like that ever again about the Davises or any other Jew. You don't know them, Maria, so it's wrong to judge them; and even if you did know a Jew and he did something wrong or something you didn't agree with, that doesn't mean they are all like that." I thought for a minute, and then added, "And it's wrong for me to call you a spoiled, rotten brat because I don't know you all that well, either. So I apologize, and maybe we can still be friends."

She sniffled and looked at me, her eyes bloodshot and her nose red as Rudolph's. "I'm sorry too, Maggie, and I really do want to be your friend. Maybe you could introduce me to Ben someday, and we could all become friends."

"Yeah, maybe; but for now let's not say anything about our fight to our parents or anyone. Agreed?" We both looked at Betsy.

"Agreed!" We all three shouted in unison and then fell back onto the bed in laughter. Suddenly Maria bolted upright, holding a tissue over her nose.

"Is my nose really that big?" she asked, blowing into the tissue again.

"No, Maria," I lied, "it's just an ordinary nose like everyone else's." I glared hard at Betsy, silencing her giggles.

There was a knock on the cabin door as Mrs. Catelli stuck her head in. "Girls, we're getting ready to go ashore. If you're going to do any diving off the bow, you need to come now." We jumped up and ran up to the top deck. I got out of my shorts in a hurry and followed Maria as she dove head first into the cool, clear waters of Lake Sharon.

The remainder of the afternoon was far more pleasant than the beginning of the day. As we were packing up to leave, Mrs. Catelli invited us to stop in at their house for a light supper, leftovers from their Friday night meal. My mother agreed, and as we left the lake, she commented on how wonderful the day turned out and that she was pleased to see her girls getting along so well with Maria. I held up my finger and shushed Betsy as we giggled to ourselves in the backseat.

CHAPTER THIRTEEN

At the Catelli mansion, we enjoyed a nice meal of beef stew and cornbread, a real Southern treat prepared by their cook the day before. As my parents waited on the patio with Mr. Catelli for their cake and coffee, Mrs. Jacobsen suddenly appeared carrying a tray of coffee, cake, and pastries; Mrs. Catelli was right on her heels.

"Look who I found out in the kitchen, for goodness' sake!" she exclaimed. Taking a seat next to my mother, she looked pleased to show off her hired help. "Margie, if you are ever planning to give a dinner party, let me know; Mrs. Jacobsen does catering as well." I chuckled to myself at the idea of my mom needing anyone to cater a party for her. *This lady has never seen my mother in the kitchen. If she can feed and entertain forty or more family members at Thanksgiving, I think she can handle some din-*

ner party! I glanced at my mom, my heart swelling with pride.

"I have special treats in the kitchen for the children," Mrs. Jacobsen announced and then turned to Maria. "Bring your friends and come with me." We followed Maria and found trays of cinnamon buns and mugs of piping hot chocolate all ready and waiting. I was impressed!

I took an instant liking to Mrs. Jacobsen, and while the others sat at the snack bar enjoying their sweets, I walked over to the sink where she was washing a mound of dirty dishes. "You sure do work hard, Mrs. Jacobsen," I said, hoping to start a friendly conversation.

She smiled at me and said simply, "Work is not hard, child; work is joy, reward. We work because we are able."

I noticed a strong foreign accent right away. "I don't work for fun," I said matter-of-factly. "I work because I will get into trouble if I don't."

Mrs. Jacobsen laughed. "It is all how you look at it. You see, there was a time when my Fritz had no work, and we had no money. We lost everything. So now I work, and am glad for it!"

Not being able to stand it for another minute, I had to ask, "Where are you and Mr. Jacobsen from?"

She hesitated momentarily, looking carefully over her shoulder, and then answered softly, "We are from old country. We come here many years ago from Romania. Mr. Catelli think we be Germans come from Germany, but no. He think we get on big boat and come to America for land of opportunity, but no." She checked once more for intruders into her conversation with me and then lowered her head closer to mine and said, "We come to escape the Nazis!"

I couldn't breathe; I couldn't think. I looked at her in disbelief, and awe at the same time. *Why was she telling me this?* Surely this was a well-kept secret that the Catellis were unaware of. The other kids were licking their fingers and reaching for more sticky buns. Mrs. Jacobsen went to refill their mugs with chocolate, leaving me standing at the sink, my mouth hanging open. *Romania?* According to my history books, Romanians were usually dark headed and dark skinned, gypsies, as they were generally referred to by the rest of the world. Mrs. Jacobsen was fair skinned, with hints of light reddish-brown hair peaking through strands of gray and white. *But hey, what do I know? I've never even met anyone who wasn't born in America.* Mrs. Jacobsen picked up the coffee pot and started out to the patio. "I be right back," she said, winking at me. Suddenly it hit me! *Was she a Jew? A Jew working right here under Mr. Catelli's nose, and he never suspected it? Why else would her heritage need to be kept secret? Of course, I guess he could hate Romanians too. If she is Jewish, it can only mean one thing; that she and Mr. Jacobsen must have narrowly escaped the horrors of the Nazi concentration camps by coming here to this country.* I needed to know more.

Mrs. Jacobsen returned to the kitchen and to the pile of dirty dishes. I found a towel and started wiping them dry as she handed them to me, listening intently to her every word.

"Mr. Jacobsen and I come here to America with nothing but the clothes on back and one tiny piece of paper with address: 14 East Brooklyn, America. It is where my cousin Sasha and husband, he dead now, live and work in shirt factory. We go to work with them and save all we can to make our own way in America. After many years we come here with money in hand enough to buy small house from Mr. Catelli, but he say no, house not good enough for Jacobsens and he have bigger house—this house. We no think so good; we say yes we want big house and give him all our money. But in 1954, Mr. Jacobsen lose job when factory he work at in city shut down. We already buy house from Mr. Catelli, but he take it back. He say it was to save our credit. What credit, I ask you? We never have no credit! No, we pay for everything we get. But big house too much for my Fritz to pay, so we finance in part with Mr. Catelli. He good to us; let us come to work after we move out, but my Fritz, he no can work now. He very sick with cancer in lung. I lose him soon, I think. One day I think to tell Mr. Catelli, 'We are Yahudim! Jews!' But I hear him yelling about Jews living in neighborhood of Mr. Sanders, and I know for sure he no like Jews. I feel in my heart I must tell him, but I fearful. He good man to work for, pay on time, so we no have to wait for money. I no want to find other work, maybe not be so lucky, but I hear him say bad things about Jews, and I want to say, 'Ha! I am Jew!'" Soapsuds flew around the kitchen as she raised her hands high up out of the dish water, gesturing emphatically.

I smiled at her, enjoying her enthusiastic disposition. *Mr. Catelli would be a fool to let her go just because she was Jewish, but after the things I heard him say to my father about the Davises, I don't doubt that his own foolish pride will eventually cost him the best cook and housekeeper in the South.*

"You know what my Fritz do before coming to America to work in shirt factory? He be Professor Fritz Jacobsen, and he teach many young students in great university in our own land, Romania!" She smiled as she put away the last of the dishes.

It was time to leave. I gave Mrs. Jacobsen a hug to which she clung securely for several minutes. Quietly, I reassured her not to worry; her secret was safe with me. I hoped to come back and tell her all about Ben and the things he had taught me about being Jewish and about the Torah, but it would have to wait. But then, in our last few minutes alone, I pulled my *chai* necklace from inside my shirt to show her. She held it in her worn and wrinkled hands for a brief moment and then looked at me, eyes beaming with tears and said simply, "Life!"

As we drove home, Betsy asleep across the back seat with her head in my lap, I thought about the Jacobsens and how hard their life must have been, leaving their home and family in Romania to escape a tyrant, coming to America for freedom and justice, only to lose yet another home, and then to end up serving the very man who took it away from them, and being thankful for the opportunity to work for him.

I have a lot to learn about forgiveness, I thought. Ben, Mrs. Jacobsen, even Maria, all had taught me valuable lessons in forgiveness. Now it was time for me to do the same. I have to find a way to teach Maria Catelli about the true nature of these Jewish people and the love they have for *El Shaddai*, the Almighty God, and to discover for myself why her father hates them so, and maybe even try to help him forgive whatever wrong they may have done him, whether actual or perceived in his mind. I was anxious to see Ben and tell him all about Mrs. Jacobsen, but first, I knew I needed to talk to my father.

Chapter Fourteen

"Dad, have you got a minute? We need to talk." I started out slowly and carefully. I didn't want this to turn into a fight, and I didn't want my father thinking I was sticking my nose into his business, but the pressure to evict the Davises was affecting everyone in the family, and it needed to be resolved. Dad had gone back to work at the plant, and ever since the trip to the lake, things seemed to be better between him and Mr. Catelli. But I'd heard him telling my mother that Catelli was giving him until the end of the month to get rid of the Davises. I needed to find out if he had done that yet, and if not, I was determined to find a way to talk him out of it or to at least stall him until I could figure out a solution. I couldn't bear the thought of losing Ben, and if they had to move away, I felt sure it would be far away, not just to a nearby neighborhood. I sat down across from my father at the kitchen table.

He looked up from his newspaper, studying my face briefly. "What's on your mind, Maggie?" he asked as he laid his paper aside, giving me his full attention.

I cleared my throat and began. First I told him how much I enjoyed the trip to Lake Sharon, and that I was wrong to think it wouldn't be any fun. I went on to tell him about the fight I'd had with Maria and how we'd made up in the end and that it looked as if we might become friends after all. I waited for him to say something, but he sat quiet, so I continued. I told him that I didn't understand why everyone hated Jewish people and that the more I learned about them the harder it was to understand. I didn't mention meeting Ben at the tree house or the beautiful silver charm I now wore inside my shirt next to my heart. I almost told him about Mrs. Jacobsen being a Jew, but I remembered my promise to her just before the words flew out of my mouth.

"Daddy, I know you think I'm just a kid, and well, maybe I am in some ways, but I'm also grown up in ways that you haven't acknowledged; like, for instance,

I think I'm plenty old enough to stay home alone all day and take care of myself, and I think I should be included in some of the decisions that involve the whole family. Also, I think it's time you explain to me why you think it's okay for Mr. Catelli to tell us who we can rent our house to and who we can and can't have for neighbors. It's not that I don't respect him, Dad; I just don't see where he had the right, that's all." Now it was my turn to be quiet and see where this was going to go. *I'll either get my answer, or I'll get sent to my room. Either way, I'll have my answer.*

My father got up from the table slowly and crossed the kitchen to the counter where the coffee pot had just finished perking. He poured a fresh cup of hot, black liquid into a mug, mixed in some cream, and then stood there for a minute, looking out the window at the little white house next door. I sat quietly, knowing it would be disastrous to rush him into this. Presently he returned to the table and sat down. One more hearty gulp of coffee and he was ready to talk.

"All right, Maggie, I guess you're right; it's time." He took a deep, steady breath and began. "Right after you were born I started looking for a place to move you and your mother to get us out of that cramped little apartment downtown. One of the guys at the plant told me that Mr. Catelli owned a few houses west of town and suggested I go talk to him about renting one. I had never even spoken to the plant owner face to face, but I figured if I was ever going to get us a house, I would need to go see him. As it turned out, he did have a house to rent, the little white one next door. Your mother and I drove over the next day to look at it, and by the weekend we were moving in. I found out later that Mr. Catelli owned several more houses on this street, including the one we live in now."

I thought this over for a minute then asked, "How did we end up owning the white house and then buying this one too?"

"We rented for a while. Then one day Mr. Catelli came to me and said that he wanted to sell the little house and that we would have to move, unless, of course, we were interested in buying it. I told your mom, and she didn't want to move, so we made him an offer on the house. The problem was that we didn't have credit with the bank to buy a house, so Mr. Catelli financed it for us. That means that we made payments to him instead of a bank; he held the deed on the property. It seemed like a good idea at the time, like he was doing us a really big favor.

"We eventually became a little better established, and then when your sister was on the way, we decided to look for a bigger house. There was a note posted on the bulletin board at work that Catelli was selling off a few houses, and this was one of them. We came over to look at it, and you and your mom fell in love with it; so I went to my boss and made him an offer on the house. Once everything was agreed upon, your mom and I realized we wouldn't have to sell the old house if Mr. Catelli held the note on this one as well. He was happy with the arrangement; more interest for him, and we didn't have to go to the bank. So Mr. Catelli owns the mortgages on both our houses, and if things don't go the way he wants them to, he will demand payment in full, and we could be out on the street. It isn't right, but my hands are tied. I don't make enough money to qualify for a bank loan on two houses, but if I don't get the Davises to move out, I either find a bank that will loan me enough to pay off Catelli, or we lose it all. I thought renting out the little house was the way to go, but now with Mr. Catelli's prejudices against the Jews, he's bound and determined to force me to kick them out, or else. The man's got a right to his own mind, but with him being my boss, I just can't risk losing my job over this mess. Getting laid off a week was just a warning." He finished his coffee and took the cup to the sink. I followed him.

"Dad, there's got to be something we can do. Mr. Catelli can't threaten us like that, can he?"

"He can, and he will, Maggie. He hates those people with a passion and nothing is going to change that. I either do what he says, or it's just a matter of time until he fires me from the plant and sics the law on us, forcing us out into the street. I don't know what my rights are or even if I have any. The agreement between Catelli and us was just that, an agreement. I mean, sure, I signed papers and all that, but I don't know if they were ever recorded at the courthouse, and Catelli has always taken care of the taxes every year and just taken it out of my pay. I thought it was a fine arrangement. Now I'm not so sure."

"Daddy, maybe we should get a lawyer to help us so Mr. Catelli can't force us to get rid of the Davises or threaten you with losing your job. I'm sure there are some good lawyers downtown. Couldn't you and Mom go talk to one of them?"

"Everything takes money, sweetheart, and that's something I don't have much of. Catelli knows that; that's why he can do what he does. He owns Charlie Ross's house, two other plant supers,' and even O'Malleys' down the street. We all have to toe the line."

"So that's what the fishing trip to the lake was all about and all those fancy Sunday dinners! He was just trying to butter you up so you would do what he says, see things his way, right?" I was angry but felt sorry for my dad. He worked so hard, but times hadn't always been favorable for him moneywise, and he and Mom had had to struggle. *It's no wonder that when someone like Mr. Catelli comes along with money to burn, that people like us are easy to buy.*

"Yeah, but there's more to it than that, and I'm not too sure I should be telling you this, you just being a kid and all, but I've gone this far, so here goes. Mr. Catelli is part of a large organization that believes that white people are superior to anyone of color, and you're either Christian or you're heathen, which is why he hates Jews. I don't agree, but for the sake of my home and job, I was trying to comply with his demands. So I tried to convince myself that maybe Catelli was right, the Jews had to go. But the fishing trip did it for me."

"How do you mean, Dad? Did he threaten you?"

"No, not in so many words at least. Actually, he offered me a promotion, provided I got rid of the Davises and joined his exclusive organization." My father looked at me for a moment, and then looked away. "It's called the Ku Klux Klan, Maggie, the KKK. Have you ever heard of them?"

Have I heard of them? They are the ones responsible for burning down businesses and hanging people off the North Street Bridge! They burn crosses in people's yards and throw rocks through windows! I couldn't get the words past my throat. I choked out a cough as I tried to speak, grabbing the edge of the counter to steady myself.

"Oh my God, Daddy, you wouldn't do that, would you? Everyone who lives in the South knows about the KKK. They do horrible things to people, innocent people, just because they are different somehow! It's like Hitler and Mussolini, or Genghis Khan!" I knew that what little I had learned in school was a mere fraction of the evil atrocities these men committed against mankind. "Those people are cowards and hide behind sheets and burn crosses and do their evil deeds in secret…and… and.…" I was trembling all over as hot tears ran down my face. I could not believe that we even knew someone who was a member of this despicable organization, and now I'd found out that my father worked for one, that our entire financial well-being was dependent on my dad working for a member of the Ku Klux Klan.

My father's hand was strong and reassuring on my shoulder as he comforted me. I'll talk to your mom, and then we'll decide—we will all decide what to do."

He pulled a cigarette from his shirt pocket and walked out to the backyard for a smoke. My heart was breaking for him. Fresh tears made their way down my cheeks as I watched my father struggling to do the right thing.

CHAPTER FIFTEEN

I wanted so badly to talk to Ben, so much so that I even thought about just going over and knocking on his front door. I trusted Ben's judgment and felt sure that he could help, but at the same time, I was afraid that if he knew our troubles, he would insist that his family leave and I would lose him forever.

I started to the refrigerator for a Coke when I spotted my father walking toward the fence. I went to the screen door to get a closer look when I saw to my disbelief, Mr. Davis standing on the other side of the fence, with a big welcoming smile on his face. *Oh no! Surely Dad hasn't decided to go through with evicting them! Or maybe he's just collecting the rent money. No, that can't be it; renters always paid on the first of the month; that's still two weeks away! Two weeks! If Dad is telling Mr. Davis they have to move, then I will have only two more weeks to spend with*

Ben! I would signal him tonight to meet me at the tree house. *I don't care if I do get into trouble*, I thought. *I have to spend as much time with him as I can!*

I watched through the screen door, tucked well out of sight of the two men. I wanted to get closer to hear what they were saying but didn't want to appear too nosey, so I stayed out of sight in the kitchen. They seemed cordial enough, no one raising his voice or thrashing his arms about. I thought of Mrs. Jacobsen and the flying soapsuds. *Jewish people seem to be very expressive*, I decided. *Either that or they are just easily excitable.* My thoughts wandered back to Ben and his big, happy smile, seeing him in my mind on that first day we met at the fence, looking so tall and handsome, eager to make new friends, and me, backward and shy, scared to death to look him eye to eye. *And I thought he was the weird one*, I chuckled to myself.

I must have been daydreaming because suddenly my dad was standing on the back porch steps looking at me through the screen. "Maggie, come out here for a minute, please."

A little flutter rose from my stomach as I slowly opened the door and stepped out onto the porch. His face didn't give away any sign of anger or frustration; if anything he seemed more at ease than before when we were talking in the kitchen. I prayed that this would not have anything to do with Ben. I followed my father over to the fence where Mr. Davis was standing.

"Maggie, this is Mr. Joe Davis; he's Ben's father. Mr. Davis, this is my daughter, Mary Margaret." I winced at the use of my full name. "Maggie," he quickly corrected himself.

I reached across the fence, politely taking the older gentleman's extended hand. "Nice to meet you, Mr. Davis." I immediately noticed an unusual marking on his forearm just above his wrist, like a number perhaps, but in a different language than ours, but his sleeve was only rolled back to that point, covering the rest of whatever it was. Suddenly I remembered—*Auschwitz! The tattooed identification mark of a condemned Jew.* I felt privileged to meet this man—a true Holocaust survivor. His handshake was firm and boisterous, how I imagined it would be like to shake hands with the president.

"Mary Margaret, what a beautiful name for a charming young lady! I count it an honor and a blessing to meet you and now call you my friend." He bowed slightly, looking at me eye to eye. He had thick, bushy gray eyebrows and lots of wrinkles. His hair was thin and curled slightly around his ears, and as he bent forward, I could see a small dark cap sitting farther back on his head. He was a nice-looking man but lean and awkwardly built, like someone whose backbone was crooked. I had a hard time thinking of him as Ben's father instead of his grandfather. I didn't know what else to say, so I looked at my dad for direction. He seemed pleased that I conducted myself so mannerly.

Mr. Davis released my hand and looked at my father. "So, Mr. Ted Sanders, it seems we have a dilemma on our hands, do we not?"

Dad must have already told him that he and his family were going to have to move out. I was mortified! *Why would he drag me out here to hear this, knowing how I felt about these people?* "Dad, you didn't tell him that they have to—" But that's as far as I got.

"Maggie," my father spoke gently, but with confidence, "Mr. Davis has a good friend who happens to be a lawyer, and he is going to get us an appointment to see him. I told him everything, Maggie." His eyes glistened with tears as he spoke. "He says his friend will most likely waive the usual attorney's fees, simply because he wants to see men like Mr. Catelli brought to justice, putting an end to all this hatred. He works with other people who have been threatened by the KKK and other racist organizations; some are Jews like himself and Mr. Davis, some are Negros, some gypsies, and some are even just everyday people like us."

I looked at Mr. Davis. He reached over the fence and patted my arm. "Now, I'm not promising it will go the way we want it to," he said soberly. "We have already been through so much, and I don't mean just the Jews! Your father has suffered at the hands of this man, Mr. Catelli, for some time now. We must pray and ask Adonai to lead us. Then we will go see Arthur Cohen, my friend the lawyer!"

Mr. Davis looked especially satisfied that he was able to help my father, and my father looked genuinely pleased that he had confided in Mr. Davis. As the two men stood talking over the fence, making plans to go into town together to meet with the lawyer, I slipped around behind my dad to the giant old oak and climbed the ladder to my tree house. I had some talking to do myself, but in private.

Seated on the old boat cushion, I pulled my silver *chai* necklace from beneath my shirt and clasped it in my hands as I bowed my head. I thanked God that he had indeed heard my prayers, and I promised that I would come to him first from now on whenever I was in trouble. I thanked him for my new friends, Ben Davis, Maria Catelli, and Mrs. Jacobsen, and I promised I would not abandon my old friend Sarah O'Malley, but that I would try to help her understand that Jewish people were just that—people who deserved our respect like anyone else. The little charm that I held between my fingers reminded me that life is precious, and never to be abused or taken for granted. Maybe Mr. Catelli would come to see that for himself someday, but for now his fate was in the hands of the people who make the laws, and of Almighty God.

Glancing out the little tree house window into the Davis's backyard, I spotted Ben sitting on the stoop of his porch. I waved; he waved back. A warm smile spread across my tear-streaked face. *You have your work cut out for you, Yaakov ben David. You must teach me everything about your people because I am your friend and I want to know.*

CHAPTER SIXTEEN

I sat nervously on the edge of the black leather sofa in the waiting room of the law office of Mr. Cohen, trying to busy myself with the aimless act of reading the fine print on the many awards and diplomas that decorated the walls of the small, downtown office. Most of them were too far for me to see from where I sat, causing me to strain my eyes until they teared up. I quickly tired of the game and looked around for a magazine. On the large coffee table in front of the sofa was a copy of the *Jerusalem Post*. I picked it up but then realized the only thing I could actually read was the title of the paper; everything else was written in Hebrew.

Instinctively I reached inside my shirt collar for my necklace. I had learned from Ben that the two Hebrew letters that made up the charm were a chet and a yud, but I still had trouble saying the word *chai*. It sounded different when Ben said it. On the front page of the paper was a picture of an old army tank and a burned-out Jeep. Of course I couldn't read the caption, but I imagined it said something like "Trouble stirring in the Middle East" or maybe even "Many people die every day on the road to Jerusalem." I tossed the paper back on the coffee table. *Someday I will be able to speak this language,* I said to myself, *and then I can read this paper and learn all about Israel.* I looked across the room at Ben. He had been sitting quietly reading a book from the moment we arrived at Mr. Cohen's office earlier this morning. I could see from the letters on the binding that it was in Hebrew. As if feeling my eyes upon him, he looked up and grinned. I was glad he hadn't volunteered to sit beside me on the sofa. True, my feelings for Ben were growing stronger by the day, but even still, I couldn't quite bring myself to think of him in terms of an actual boyfriend. He smiled again and then went back to his book. I think he felt the same way about me. We were best friends. We would enjoy that for as long as it lasted before moving to the next level of our relationship.

The office door opened suddenly, and Mr. Cohen walked into the waiting room, followed by my father and mother and Mr. Davis. Ben stood to his feet, politely offering my mother his chair. She sat down as the three men talked quietly with each other. Mr. Cohen nodded in apparent agreement, and then the two men shook hands with him, indicating that the meeting was over and it was time to leave. I joined my mom as she stood and moved closer to the door.

I knew this was not the proper time for questions, so I slid into the back seat of our station wagon and waved good-bye to Ben and Mr. Davis through the passenger window as they drove away. I didn't know how long I could keep quiet. This had been a trying week for my parents, the Davises, and me, waiting for the appointment with the attorney and trying all the while to remain calm in the face of turmoil.

Finally my dad spoke up. "Maggie, your mother and I appreciate your patience and we know you have lots of questions for us, but we feel that it would be best to go home and rest a while before we get into a discussion. We still have to pick Betsy up from the sitters, and your mother wants to get lunch on the table."

He glanced at me through his rear view mirror. I tried to smile, but I knew it wasn't very convincing.

"Okay, Dad, whatever you say is fine by me." No use in arguing. I would just have to wait it out.

As Mom settled Betsy in front of the television for some cartoons, I cleared away lunch dishes and wiped the kitchen table. Dad still sat at his place at the table, his lunch untouched, his checkbook lying next to his plate. I wondered if the attorney had charged my father a fee after all, creating an additional burden on him. "Daddy, aren't you going to finish your lunch?" I hesitated before reaching for his plate.

"I'll eat later, honey," he said without looking up. I left the plate and went back to the sink to wash the remaining dishes. "Maggie, I don't mean to ignore you. I just have a lot on my mind right now. Come sit down for a minute." I went back to the table and sat down. Mom walked into the kitchen and took a seat next to my father. *So, here we are,* I thought. *Let's get this thing out in the open.* He closed his checkbook and pushed it aside. A grim look came over my mother's face, and she looked away. "Margie, there's just nothing we can do; there's not a dime extra this month."

"I know, Ted," she replied sadly. "I was just hoping we could pay the man a little something to show our gratitude. But it's okay. I'm sure he will understand." Suddenly she reached across the table and patted my hand. "It is going to be fine, Maggie. Stop worrying!" I forced a smile for her sake and then looked back at my dad. The expression on his face was not nearly as reassuring as the sweetness in my mother's voice.

"Mr. Cohen says there's not really much we can do at the moment. Not that we have to do anything, I mean like force the Davises out on the street, but we don't have any grounds for legal action against Catelli. So far all he has done is talk, and there's no law against a self-righteous bigot running his mouth." A sideways glance at my mom told me she disapproved of his choice of words, but she made no effort to correct him as he continued. "If things get worse, and I feel sure they will, then we'll see. Mr. Cohen assured us that he will defend us at any rate and at no cost. That is very generous of him, and I have no doubt it is because of his loyalty to Joe Davis. Either way, I'm grateful."

"So that's it? Mr. Catelli gets away with everything and the Davis family continues to suffer? How is that fair, Dad?"

My father did not answer my question. He simply got up from the table, placed his uneaten meal on the counter, and went in and joined Betsy on the sofa in front of the television. Mom looked at me sadly and then folded her arms on the table and laid her head on her arms. No answers, no justice, no satisfaction. Nothing.

The ringing of the telephone jolted me from my thoughts. Mom jumped up from the table and ran into the living room, where my dad had just picked up the receiver. I followed her, listening closely as my father spoke.

"Yeah, this is Ted Sanders. What? What did you say? Who is this? Hey, buddy, you don't call my house and use that kind of filthy language, you hear me? Hello? Hello?" He slammed the receiver back into the cradle and looked at my mom. "The nerve of that guy!"

Mom moved a little closer to my father. "Ted, who was that?" Dad's face was twisted into a frightening combination of rage and contempt. His fists were clenched tight and unyielding. He walked over and stared out the window. Mom didn't move, but neither did she take her eyes off him.

"Some fool idiot who thinks he can call here and say whatever he wants and threaten my family." Reaching in his shirt pocket, he took out a cigarette and lit it right there in our living room, his eyes scanning the street in front of our house.

A black, late model sedan drove past the house unusually slow. I moved in closer to my mother. Mom began to tremble, tears welling up in her eyes. She looked at me. "Maggie, take your sister upstairs, please."

"But, Mom—," I started to protest.

"Maggie! Go!" my dad shouted at me.

I grabbed my sister's hand, yanking her up off the sofa, and ran upstairs to my room. I hated missing the action, even if it was just because of a phone call, but I knew I had to trust my parents and I knew their number one priority was to protect me and my sister. We sat on the side of my bed and waited. I glanced over at the top of my bureau at the menorah. *What would Ben do right now? Would he just sit here, helpless and afraid? Or would he reach out to that higher power that he believed in*

135

and trusted more than anything in his life? I walked over to the menorah and ran my fingers over its surface. "Father God, show me what to do," I prayed softly. As if a supernatural force had suddenly surrounded me, I reached for the menorah, took Betsy's hand, and started back downstairs. Slipping through the kitchen undetected by my parents, I found a book of matches in the silverware drawer and walked out to the back porch. Digging around in a box on the shelf over the washing machine where mom kept her storm candles, I counted out seven scraggly, mismatched candles. *No matter*, I told myself. *God knows what is in my heart.* We ran across the backyard to the oak tree. As we started up the ladder to the tree house, I spotted Ben in his back-yard, tossing a stick toward his dog, Sparky. I waved at him just as he turned in my direction. Immediately, he dropped the stick, ran to the side of his yard, and hopped the fence. Without a word, he climbed the ladder and joined Betsy and me as we sat on the floor, the menorah in the center.

"What's up?" Ben asked, smiling at Betsy as if to say, "Welcome to the club."

"We need you to pray Ben, pray hard! Something bad has happened. I don't have any details, but trust me, it is real bad. I don't know what else to do."

Ben picked up the matches and pulled one out of the pack while I stuffed the little pink, yellow, and blue candles into the cups of the menorah branches. Unconsciously I placed the only white candle in my hand into the center cup. Ben struck the match and lit the Shamash. Betsy reached for my hand as she held her breath. Finally all seven candles were lit. I wondered if I needed to tell Ben about the phone call and the black car driving past our house so he would know what to pray about, but as he closed his eyes I realized that it would not be necessary. As he began to speak in the Hebrew language, I truly believed I was experiencing a miracle—I understood.

YVAREKH'KHA ADONAI V'YISHMEREKHA.

YA'ER ADONAI PANAV ELEIKHA VICHUNEKKA.

YISSA ADONAI PANAV ELEIKHA V'YASEM I'KHA SHALOM.

I knew now that from this day forward the Lord's blessing was upon us. No matter the threats, no matter the hate, no matter the bigotry and racism, no matter who or what posed itself as an enemy to our families, we would have shalom—peace.

May the Lord bless you and keep you.

May the Lord make His face to shine upon you and show you His favor.

May the Lord lift up His face toward you and give you peace.

The End.